PRAISE FOR CURTIS WHITE'S FICTION

"His take on the medium is winningly idiosyncratic; Curtis White writes out of an admirable intellectual sophistication combined with viscerality, pain, and humor."

- JOHN BARTH -

"Curtis White is a one-man band, a whirling dervish, a devil who speaks in tongues, a master of bewitchments, parodies, and dazzling tropes."

- PAUL AUSTER -

"Curtis White's fiction presents a scintillant, ironic surface, one that is barely able to contain the bleakness of American *fin-de-siècle* exhaustion, which latter is his essential theme."

- GILBERT SORRENTINO -

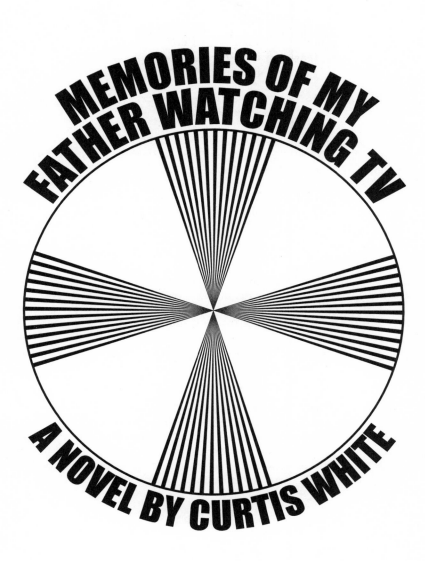

MEMORIES OF MY FATHER WATCHING TV

A NOVEL BY CURTIS WHITE

Dalkey Archive Press

Stills from *The Third Man* by permission of the British
Film Institute.

The following stories previously appeared in these publications:
"Combat" and "Manic Maverick," in *The Iowa Review* and *Postmodern American Fiction: A Norton Anthology,* "TV Scandal," in *The Coe Review,* "Have Gun—Will Travel," in *The Santa Monica Review,* "Bonanza," in *After Yesterday's Crash: the Avant-Pop Anthology* (Viking), "Sea Hunt," in *The Exquisite Corpse,* and "Highway Patrol," in *Nobodaddies.*

Library of Congress Cataloging-in-Publication Data:

White, Curtis, 1951-
Memories of my father watching TV / by Curtis White. — 1st ed.
p.   cm.
ISBN 1-56478-189-5 (alk. paper)
I. Title.
PS3573.H4575M46   1998
813'.54—dc21   97-51440
CIP

In a book full of pirated passages, the author particularly wishes to acknowledge the "samples" taken from Paul Driver's "A Third Man Cento," in *Sight and Sound,* Winter 1989.

This publication is partially supported by a grant from the Illinois Arts Council, a state agency.

Dalkey Archive Press
Illinois State University
Campus Box 4241
Normal, IL 61790-4241

Our Scene

The defining childhood memory of my father is of a man (but not just a man, of course; it is *my father*—young, handsome, capable!) reclined on a dingy couch watching TV. Watching TV and ignoring the chaos around him, a chaos consisting almost entirely of me and my sisters fighting. Like most brothers and sisters, we fought about everything—who got the last, largest or best (whatever that could mean) piece of fudge, for example. Or the chaos was of a different kind. It was Winny, the younger of my two sisters, passing rapidly and continuously back and forth before the TV, through my father's view, moving from point A to point B. That's how desperate she was to be seen. More desperate, even, than a compulsive who must keep her hands clean, clean. But my father never seemed to notice. Winny might as well have been the infinitesimal black strip of celluloid that separates discreet images on film. He could see easily through the haze her to-and-froing created. Janey, sister number two and nearly my own age, stood obliquely to Dad's side, posed like a Roman orator, holding forth endlessly on nothing in particular. She would argue eloquently of the injustice of a house with heat in one room only. Or she would complain, as I once heard my grandmother complain (her mind in the squeeze of senile dementia), about the immorality of cowboy serials in general and *Gunsmoke* in particular. Issues of similar profundity. Janey's speaking voice went out like sonar, never finding what it was looking for. But neither did this act gather Dad's attention. Me, I stood behind him, completely out of view. Thus my unique strategy: I didn't need to be seen in order to be. But if, dear Father, you would happen to turn around, what a feat you'd witness! A true spectacle! Your own son flipping Kraft miniature marshmallows into the air and catching them in his mouth. A whole bag flipped and eaten without missing one! Yes, I was the family's phenom.

Imagine this scene:

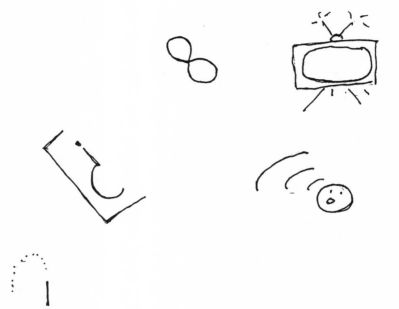

Winny=& (like a shuttle)
Janey=O (like a great mouth)
Chris=! (like a marvel)
Dad=? (like an enigma)

And the TV? It is an oracle. It is speaking to us. It has something very important to say. Tonight it is presenting . . . Our Shows.

MEMORIES OF MY FATHER WATCHING TV

GLOOM

TV SCANDAL

My father's involvement in a pair of famous scandals, both associated with the early traumas of television, needs one more rehearsal. I am not interested in excusing my father for his part in these national humiliations. I mean only to say that the accepted, conventional version of his participation in our mass media calamities is wrong. Stupid. Completely to the side, even if a parallel side, of the truth. The irritation is that countless popular histories have made the American public so familiar with one version of his guilt that those histories have achieved the status of common sense. Was my father a cheat and traitor? Did we like Ike? Was Dick tricky?

What needs pointing out, even if his son must do it, is that there is a deeper (and inevitably "psychological") way of understanding his decisions. Doesn't anyone think it relevant to point out that during the Great Depression (aptly named) my father was abandoned by his own father? We shouldn't need a psychoanalyst to see the consequences of that on the immature self-esteem of a five-year-old boy. Deprived of the soothing presence of a loving father, and deprived of the food and physical comfort (the Kleinian "good breast") a responsible father might be expected to provide, my father was placed at the top of a psychic chute, the fall from which leads to humiliation, shame and powerlessness. No hope.

For me, it all comes down to this: why aren't these problems and questions, imponderable as they may be, at least relevant to my father's notorious case? Why are we allowed only the idiotically naked presentation of "the facts": my father as the moral metaphysician of all postwar cynicism and national self-defeat? I don't think it's fair, but then I am his son. And obviously my father himself might object, but, unhappily, his attention has not been distracted from our television set since the early 1960s, so it's difficult to know exactly what he might think. Nonetheless, I feel some sympathy for the guy. Or, perhaps you will say, I feel pity for myself. For I, too, like my father, am one of those for whom the most distant jagged star is something I've caught my sleeve on.

All I ask is that we open again the question of whether my father is the failed self, the worthless self, the tragic "modern man" he is so often depicted as being.

Scandal

In the 1950s, in the years following the famous McCarthy investigations (which a spellbound America watched unravel in their very own living rooms during the live broadcasts of the Army-McCarthy hearings), my father was thrown, like the rest of America, into a contradictory and futile effort to be something other than insidious. Americans didn't wish to think of themselves as cruel and malicious; they wanted to be generous (not that one could always tell the difference). So life-on-TV came up with "microscope-on-misery" programming like *Queen for a Day*. There, an impoverished mother of legions, married to a landscaper paid in grass clippings, competed with another mother, each of whose children had been born without important body parts. The contestant who received the loudest and most sustained audience applause won the day's prizes. LET'S HEAR IT FOR MRS. X! (Grass clippings shower down around her, piling at her feet. The applause meter leaps, quivers, sags, rebounds.) AND NOW MRS. Y. (She holds up her twelfth child, who wriggles two stumps for arms. The applause is not so grand.) The winner takes all the goodies. The loser, Mrs. Y, goes home, doubly lost, to a world of broken children.

Neither did Americans wish any longer to seem to hate intellectuals, or "eggheads" as Adlai Stevenson's supporters had been dubbed. These were the Sputnik years, after all. There was national need for someone to be smart. Americans simply wished intelligence to be more common. As Charles

Revson, president of Revlon cosmetics and corporate sponsor of *The $64,000 Question*, put it, "We're trying to show the country that the little people are really very intelligent and knowledgeable. That's why the quiz shows have caught on—because of the little people." Yes, the little people—and big money.

Unhappily, like all entertainment programs, what the quiz shows really dealt in was illusion, the illusion, in this case, of imagining that the "common person" was smart.

The shows—*Twenty-One, Tic-Tac-Dough, Dotto,* and *The $64,000 Question,* as well as more implausible quizzes like *Break the $250,000 Bank, Hold That Note, Name That Tune, Do You Trust Your Wife?, Treasure Hunts, Twenty Steps to a Million, Two for the Money, Top Dollar, Take It or Leave It, Double or Nothing, Strike It Rich, You're on Your Own, Winky Dinky and You, Your Blood Our Cash, Sing It, What's My Line?, Hi-Lo, What You Won't Do for Money, I've Got a Secret, High Finance, Number Please, 100 Grand, Lucky Partners, Get Out of Debt, Giant Step, Dough Re Mi, Go Back to Oklahoma, Big Moment, Big Payoff, Big Board, Big Squeeze, Big Knockers, Big Surprise, Big Deal, Anybody Can Win,* and *Everybody Loses*—these shows were all vaguely sleazy. The sets were compounded of beaverboard and sequins, liberally decorated with the name of the sponsor. There was the usual pretty girl (*The $64,000 Question*'s girl was actually named Lynn Dollar) whose function was to escort contestants onto the stage and to confuse sexual and commodity lust. The host was always a kindergarten egomaniac whose presence made it impossible to imagine not being "thrilled to be on the show." He combined enthusiasm and depravity.

Of course, as we all know, these quiz shows suffered a terrible scandal when it was discovered that game producers were feeding contestants answers in "warm up sessions" in order to control the drama of the contests and to make sure a "boring" contestant didn't dominate the program for weeks. Thus, the apparently good-hearted effort of television to display and applaud the intelligence of America's ordinary people turned into just the opposite. Americans were left with the feeling that they'd been conned by shysters and hucksters. TV was, as usual, just selling soap and "Love that Pink" lipstick. But what the conning showed was not the other's (corporate) evil but their own (American) stupidity. It was a self-image problem, no? Poor-little-rich-kid America, embarked on a Cold War mission for the hearts of the world, worried: "The world will not love me if I am not smart. If the world does not love me, I will always be alone. I may be smart and I may not be. But I can only be certain to appear smart if I cheat. But only stupid people cheat, and stupid people cannot cheat successfully precisely because stupid people are too stupid to pull off the difficulties of cheating. If a person could cheat successfully, he would be smart. But smart people would never cheat because smart people know that if they cheat and are caught, they will be known as frauds. The stupid/fraud is not loved by the world twice. The world's contempt is doubled. It is a game of Nothing and Double Nothing. Therefore I have no choice but to cheat." More than anything else, the fatal non-sequitur at the end of this syllogism indicates collective doom.

My father's participation in The Quiz Show scandals is one of the most humiliating memories of my youth. Mom said my sisters and I could watch Dad play a show called *Dotto* if we brushed our teeth, put on our pj's and got ready for bed. We did, eagerly, and flopped down before the tube. The ominous flickering began, and there displayed by the grey dots (which I could actually see if I put my eye right on the screen) was Dad. (Even years later I was pursued by the nonsensical question: how many dots make a dad?)

TRANSCRIBED KINESCOPE OF *DOTTO*, MAY 20, 1958

RALPH PAUL. In just a few moments, the first phone call. Stand by. You may be phoned. This may be the lucky day on which you join life-on-TV. If it is, you will win a fabulous prize. All you have to do is watch—watch those dots. *Dotto! Dotto,* the exciting new quiz game, brought to you by Colgate

Dental Cream. Fight tooth decay with Colgate while you stop bad breath all day. And here's your host for *Dotto,* Jack Narz. (fanfare)

NARZ. Hi everybody. Thank you very much. Tonight, on behalf of Colgate, may I welcome you to *Dotto.* What we do is, we have a series of dots back here which, when they are connected, form a picture, and those pictures turn into dollars for our studio contestants. And right now let's meet our first two guests. Ralph, please.

PAUL. Well, Jack, getting us off on a solid note—returning for the second day, Colgate Dental Cream welcomes back our new champion from New York, Dr. Mark Ransom, a professor of English at Columbia University and one of the most widely read and erudite men in the world.

NARZ. Terrific. Welcome back, Mr. Ransom.

RANSOM. Thank you.

NARZ. You really moiderized your last challenger. [laughter]

RANSOM. Pardon me?

NARZ. [mugging into the camera] No, pardon *me.* Pardon me my shoddy diction. You gave your last challenger a sound thumping. [general hilarity]

RANSOM. Well, the series of questions asking for the basis of Kant's distinction between Understanding and Reason in his metaphysical, moral and aesthetic philosophies was perhaps unfair to him.

NARZ. Not a bit unfair! America's common people are smart! Highly intelligent! Good adversaries for anyone. Your opponent may have been a janitor in a junior high school, but he knows philosophy too. Try him on Aristotle's hylomorphic theory of composition. Try him on Aquinas's use of the *regressus ad infinitum.* It was just his bad luck not to know Kant. But today, for you, a new challenger. Ralph.

PAUL. Won't you please welcome our new challenger, from San Lorenzo, California, Levittown West, Mr. Carl White. [applause]

NARZ. Welcome to *Dotto,* Mr. White. I understand that you are a claims adjustor. That that is your profession. You adjust claims for the Tiny Nibbles Cat Food Company in Oakland, California.

CARL. Yes, that's right.

NARZ. What exactly does a claim adjustor for cat food do?

CARL. [embarrassed] That has always been a fuzzy issue for me.

NARZ. Really? Well, what do you do when you're at work?

CARL. [shyly] I've never understood my duties very well.

NARZ. Don't people, your company's customers perhaps, come to you with claims?

CARL. What kind of claims?

NARZ. Isn't it possible that they might say the cat food was not fresh, or there were bugs, or the boxes were opened, ripped or otherwise defective?

CARL. Perhaps that's it. That sounds plausible.

NARZ. [laughing good naturedly] Just plausible? You go to work daily, correct? You must be paid regularly for something.

CARL. [a little indignant] Of course I'm paid. How else could I provide for my family? I have a wife and three children who depend on me.

NARZ. Well, it must be a very complex job and difficult to describe to non-professionals. Let's turn to one more fact about your personal life before starting our game. I'm told that—oh my—you describe yourself as a turd with a hat on? Is that right? [laughter]

RANSOM. Dear me.

CARL. [cowering] That's correct. [mumbling inaudibly, looking under his podium for his feet, gesturing] I didn't think they would actually use that information. I was just being honest with their question. They asked me how I would describe myself to someone who didn't know me. So I told them. What's so wrong about that? Now they use it against me. They use my honesty to hurt me.

NARZ. A very unusual self-description, Carl. Why do you feel this way about yourself?

CARL. There's nothing very complicated about it. I am a turd with a hat on.

NARZ. Do you think that other people see you like this?

CARL. That's why I don't let people get too close to me. Not even my own children. They only see the hat. I don't let people see that I'm all shit underneath. [audience laughs, heads shake with amazement at eccentricity of the average American]

NARZ. Very well, Carl. We'll start our first match in just a moment. Right now, a word to you folks. Do you know who was the first to put toothpaste in a tube? Colgate, that's right. And now, who was the first with an aerosol toothpaste? Colgate! Watch.

[commercial break]

NARZ. Mark and Carl, for each of you we have some Colgate Dental Cream with Gardol and Power-packed Colgate. Okay, all set now to go with our first match. Good luck, gentlemen, and would you take your positions in the *Dotto* isolation booths, please. We can hear you but you won't be able to hear each other. Remember, the sooner you identify the picture, the more money you'll make. Carl, our first category for today is mood disorders. You have your choice of 5, 8, or 10 dots. Mood disorders—

CARL. What's a mood disorder?

NARZ. [amazed] I'm sorry, Carl, I can't go into that right now. You'll just have to do your best.

CARL. Okay. Five points, then.

NARZ. Fine. And here is your question, in self-object theory, narcissistic rage occurs when . . .

CARL. Narcissistic rage occurs when that 'gleam in the other's eye' known as mirroring fails to approve, confirm and reward the self.

NARZ. For five dots that's correct! Tremendous, Carl. [applause]

CARL. Everybody knows that one.

NARZ. Now let's connect some of the dots on our board. It may be the face of a famous person or it may be a common or familiar object. Any guesses, Carl?

CARL. It looks like just a mess so far.

NARZ. Is that a guess? Is that an official guess?

CARL. No. I'll try another question for five points. I can't go any lower than five?

NARZ. No. Let me remind you again that our category is mood disorders. Specifically, hopelessness. Hopelessness. Ready?

CARL. Not really. I mean, do I have a choice? I don't see how I can get this question. This game is way too hard for me. Mr. Ransom is a college professor and a real champion. I just don't see how I can win.

NARZ. Well, audience, he really seems to know a lot about this category. [Good natured laughing. Shouts of encouragement. "Come on, idiot. At least try." "Yeah, see can you do a man's job, buddy."]

NARZ. Okay, for five points, the most distal cause in the pathway of processes that produce hopelessness depression is what, Carl?

CARL. The distal cause in hopelessness depression is negative life events exacerbated by personal inferential styles.

NARZ. Right again! [amazed applause] You're quite expert on this stuff.

CARL. Thank you.

NARZ. Well, let's see those new dots. Huh. Interesting. Any ideas, Carl?

CARL. Well, that's definitely a hat there on top or maybe a kind of sombrero. Say, is that a turd with a hat on?

NARZ. That's it! [flashing lights, bells, sirens, horns, applause] Carl, you're incredibly quick, and you are our new champion. Sorry, Mark, you're done before you've even had a chance.

RANSOM. That's okay. I know how the game works. I could never have answered those question anyway. A turd with a hat on! Who'd have guessed?

NARZ. Well, our new champion Carl White could guess! What do you think of your prospects and abilities now, Carl?

CARL. I guess I'm doing okay, Mr. Narz. But I feel like I don't deserve this success. I feel fraudulent. I think I may even have cheated. [audience in sympathy: "Nooooo."] The picture was of something we'd just talked about. Is that fair? Was that fair to Mr. Ransom?

NARZ. Don't you worry about Mr. Ransom, Carl. His total earnings on the show will exceed his professor's pay for the next ten years. Did you hear him complain? Actually, we tried to trick you! We were unfair. Think about it. After talking about turds with hats on, what's the last thing you would expect to find on our game board?

CARL. A turd with a hat on.

NARZ. Exactly. Kudos to the toughness of your insight.

CARL. [rises in booth] No. I am being inappropriately praised. You don't really admire me. You are lying to me. I should feel shame for cheating, but you praise me. This makes me very angry [tries to open door to isolation booth but it is locked]. I feel a primitive atavistic rage. Images are coming to me. I am striking you with my fist. I am hitting you in the face with objects. I hit you with the stupid dental cream product. [shaking isolation booth door]

NARZ. Well, well. Our isolation booths have a new purpose this evening, don't they audience? [audience laughs and applauds] Carl, if you are very bad, we will have to leave you locked in your booth. How would that make you feel?

CARL. [Moans. Face goes through a series of inhuman distortions each of which the audience finds funny.]

NARZ. Carl, I believe that tonight we have put you in touch with a deep underlying sense of disappointment, hurt and vulnerability that has been defended against by this show of anger.

CARL. [despondent] You're right. I've disgraced myself again. No one can love an angry person. I will be alone in this game show isolation booth forever. That is what I deserve.

Shame

The public horror over quiz shows and the fraudulent participation of otherwise honorable people like my father was best expressed by poet John Ciardi when he said, "Bah! You asked for it. This is your life. The price is right enough.

You've got no secrets. People are . . . well, never mind. But tell me, boys and girls and Federal gentlemen, has anyone had time to think of Khrushchev lately?"

Khrushchev? In 1959 my father had *only* Khrushchev on his mind.

Of course, by 1959 Khrushchev already had a prominent role in life-on-TV. He'd become a character in American consciousness, as real as Dave Garroway. He was someone who explained the world with charm at hours when the world made no sense by itself. He was funny, quick-witted, open and avuncular. He was ridiculous and yet heroic and principled; he would stand knee-deep in the middle of a muddy field in order to explain to skeptical peasants the proper way to plant potatoes. On the other hand, American politicians like McCarthy and Richard Nixon seemed made all of shadows. They had no control of their beards, and, unfortunately, facial hair meant 'villain' in TV's visual argot. So TV had gotten the great international drama backwards. The Russians wore comical hats and wanted to go to Disneyland. The Americans sent spy planes over other countries, like Gary Powers's U2, then denied it, then blustered about their rights and interests when the captured pilot was brought forward clutching girlie magazines and cyanide needles.

Something had to be done to put the white hats back on the real good guys. This project began in 1958 when the American and Soviet governments approved a cultural exchange program. The United States was to stage an exhibit in Moscow depicting the "typical" American home. This average domicile included color television, videotape, and other marvels of Western consumer technology. American strategists imagined that such an exhibit would leave the "typical" Muscovite with his borscht dripping from his beard in concentrated awe. Vice President Nixon himself would open the exhibit and meet with Khrushchev. Nixon hoped to create an event for a watchful television world. As with his Checkers speech, he was conscious of the need for an artful reality.

Nixon guided Khrushchev to a room equipped with an

RCA closed-circuit color television and Ampex videotape machine. As they entered the room, they could see themselves on a monitor. They were being taped, so they would immediately be able to see a replay of their live performance. This was the high-water mark in the history of international diplomatic narcissism. Nixon and Khrushchev stared into the monitor, waved and grinned as if they thought themselves very pretty, as if they were two little boys regarding themselves in the shiny chrome of the family toaster.

Recalling himself and the weeks of preparation for this moment, Nixon began an explanation of the technological marvels around them. Khrushchev, for his part, did not relish the role in which he was cast—a mute country bumpkin listening to explanations from the advanced West. So he interrupted.

"My friend, Mr. Nixon, why is the United States so reluctant to sign a mutual disarmament agreement?"

Nixon, understandably, found it difficult to shift from a description of the minor miracle of the clothes dryer to a defense of American imperialism. Nixon was leaning against a rail in front of a kitchen exhibit. A box of SOS soap pads sat atop a clothes dryer. Leonid Brezshnev glowered over Nixon's shoulder. Nixon stumbled desperately forward, "Have I thoroughly explained the Maytag principle of product guarantee to you, Premier Khrushchev? Are you sure you have no questions?"

"Yes, I comprehend it in all of its multiform glories and details. But why, tell me, if the United States is a peaceful power, why must you have military bases around the world? And you may not tell me they are defensive. No. That answer I will not accept. I do not believe that Manilla is a suburb of New York City."

In that case, Nixon did not know how to respond. He wanted desperately to talk about appliances. That is what he was prepared to do. He was also utterly aware of being trapped on videotape. The video camera reported everything just as it happened. This knowledge of course made Nixon self-conscious. How should a diplomat behave while in a kitchen discussing atom bombs? He had no idea. So, in a mild panic, he retreated to American cowboy politics, which had a short but potent stack of visual strategies available. He saw himself projected as Roy Rogers, Gene Autry or the Lone Ranger. He jabbed a finger into Khrushchev's chest. Nikita's eyebrows lifted in amazed amusement as Nixon's digit sunk to the first knuckle in his peasant chubbiness. This diplomacy was more than real.

"Premier Khrushchev, the United States does not need a lecture from you on the importance of world peace. If you were really concerned, you would allow the enslaved nations of the Eastern bloc to create their own futures democratically. We have our own ideas about freedom, you know. You must not be afraid of ideas. You don't know everything. So I would ask you to desist from insulting the United States of America."

In return, Khrushchev waved an aggressive finger of his own at Nixon. But it was his pinkie, not a finger that a cowboy would wave. Khrushchev was thus marked as alien. He lacked access to the authentic cowboy diplomatic vernacular.

"America may by all means continue to live under capitalism," he rejoined. "But don't inflict it upon us.

"As for your claim that I insult the good USA," he now turned directly toward the camera and grinned, "you remind me of an old Russian story." He strummed his fingers on his chest with a vaudevillian flourish. Apparently, Khrushchev was more familiar with the clownish politics of Uncle Milty. "Two passengers were travelling in a train after the 1905 revolution. The passengers were engaged in a conversation. Other people were sitting opposite listening to the conversation. One said to the other:

" 'The tsar is a fool!'

"A gendarme heard this and asked, 'How dare you call the tsar a fool!'

" 'Excuse me,' the passenger replied, 'I meant that the German tsar is a fool.'

"But the gendarme was not so easily fooled. 'I know my tsar,' he shouted, 'if anyone is a fool, it is our tsar!' "

Khrushchev added nothing to this enigmatic tale but his dollar-fifty smile.

This encounter became know as the "kitchen debate," and was the basis for Nixon's lifelong claim of "standing up" to the Russians. But when my father saw this famous scene in internatinal diplomacy, he was not impressed. He was in his angry mode. He felt that Nixon had been humiliated by the Communists. Nixon's humiliation and his strong sense of his own humiliation became one and the same. My father wanted vengeance. If only *he* could debate Khrushchev.

Then, marvellously, as if my father's psychotic notion that his thoughts influenced the external world were nothing more than the case, this debate seemed possible. Khrushchev was coming to the United States! My father began sending challenges to the Soviet delegation of the United Nations. New York and the General Assembly of the U.N. would be a good format, he suggested. Or the Grand Canyon. He mailed daily sets of instructions to the U.S. State Department. Now, you may well say that he never did really meet Khrushchev. I don't know. You may say that the purpose of the visit to our home by the FBI and Soviet security was not to finalize debate protocol, but to make sure Dad was not stalking the Premier. But the story my father told me of his encounter with the famous Nikita K. was so particular in its details that I have always been tempted to find it credible.

[Note: As I've mentioned, my father has been in a cataleptic trance before the TV since November of 1963. I think there was something hypnotic in the Kennedy funeral procession. The clip-clop of the horses in the streets of Washington D.C. The lonely despairing echo of those hooves in our little suburban home. You must realize that in spite of appearances this story was not told as stories are ordinarily told. On the porch. Over some beers. Rather, my father's coma would occasionally crack and fall open like an egg. Then he could jabber for a few moments.]

"When Khrushchev came to the U.S., Son, it was inevitable that we meet. He knew all about my life on TV. He'd even seen my game show appearances. That's the kind of thorough students of the American scene the Russians were. Not narrow idiots like our Nixon. But God knows I'd watched my share of TV. I was prepared for any encounter."

Of course, what Khrushchev had seen in my father's forlorn performances was an entire American tragedy. Consumer yearning, sexual bafflement, autocratic cruelty, and crushed pride. But Khrushchev was perhaps wrong to assume that merely experiencing the country's hypocrisy could turn people like my father against it. As he often said to me, "Butch, remember this, you only really need patriotism when your country is dead wrong!"

He continued. "Mr. K. was in the West Coast phase of his trip when I got the call. The premier would meet me in L.A. They sent a Russian military plane up to the Alameda airfield to fetch me. We arrived in Anaheim around midnight. We got in a diplomatic car and drove through that prefabricated tropical paradise straight toward Disneyland.

"But I knew, as everyone in the country knew, that Khrushchev had been told he couldn't go to Disneyland. Why should he get to go to Disneyland? That's a treat for good boys. 'Have gangsters taken over the place?' Mr. K. asked. 'What do they have there—rocket launching pads?'

"Scheming, devious Commies! He knew very well that we had rocket launching pads there and more. Why, we had Tomorrowland itself. Your future, boy!"

According to Dad, he was let out of the KGB car in an obscure corner of the park, back where the stables are. Agents had built a ladder in the dead of night and flopped it over the barbed wire fence. Over this fence Dad was popped like bundled contraband. Understand this astonishing fact: the Soviet KGB was smuggling my yankee-doodle father into Disneyland. It was a scene no whit different from what one saw at the East German border, only refracted by a new order. His face was blackened and he was given camouflaged overalls. The only difference between my father and the KGB guys was that they wore conspicuous name tags. "Hi, my name is Jimmie." "Hi, my name is Roy." They were his hosts.

They walked up the broad, desolate boulevard of Main

Street USA past the Shooting Gallery and the Silhouette Studio. They came to the hub, Disneyland's crossroads. Signs pointed to the worlds available. Adventureland. Fantasyland. Frontierland. Tomorrowland.

Jimmie turned to my father, light reflecting in his dark eastern eyes, as if the famed Disney fireworks sparkled overhead. "Well, comrade," he said, "which will it be?"

Comrade! My father felt an awful sensation. Who was he, finally? Comrade or American patriot? Was he there to assassinate Krushchev? Debate him? Or share valuable national secrets? His own identity and the fate of the entire American experiment seemed to ride on his choice.

"Tomorrowland, of course."

My father's choice was decisive, firm, in spite of the fact that he couldn't possibly understand two things about his decision. First, whichever path he chose the Premier waited for him at its end. Khrushchev reclined coquetishly in Sleeping Beauty's bed in Fantasyland; he shot hippos and grunted "DA" from the stern of the jungle cruiser in Adventureland; he was the fat kid diving into the dirty Mississip just beneath Tom Sawyer's Teetertotter Rock in Frontierland. Second, Dad couldn't possibly understand the puzzle locked in the fact that Tomorrowland would remain as it was for decade after decade. It was thus an always already dusty tomorrow he sought.

Once in Tomorrowland, they proceeded straight to the enormous Rocket to the Moon. A figure greeted them at the door dressed in a space suit and helmet with CCCP in decal over the visor. He held an American hot dog in his right hand. Was it K.? "Greetings to you from the Union of Soviet Socialist Republics." He waved the hot dog, which his helmet prevented him from eating. They entered the rocket.

Inside it was completely dark. The cosmonaut who had greeted Dad now took him by the hand as if he were a child needing guidance through a difficult and frightening place. Finally, they came to a table on which sat what appeared to be a human head, glowing. Its eyes were closed and it was motionless. My father's guide dropped his hand and went to the head. He pushed a button at the head's side and it came immediately to life. It could talk. It was fully human, and it was clearly the head of Nikita Khrushchev. There was the corpulent face, the laughing angry eyes, the fat, ascerbic tongue of the most entertaining, resourceful and loved Soviet leader. The eyes in the head burned very deep into the truths of childhood. This was a Great Moment.

The head spoke, a vague whirring and clicking floating behind his words, as if he were a clock, or as if he were a latex mask stretched taut around a solenoid core. "Skin and blood. Passion and sleep. This is our empire. We work in the shadow of a travesty. Overhead the sky changes. See? Steelwork encloses me, the incandescent imp. Burning, I would light the way for the Party."

Uncomprehending, Dad looked for assistance to his cosmonautical guide. Deep within the visor of his space helmet a pale smile radiated. It was without question the disembodied Cheshire cat grin of foreign treachery.

"I have some questions for you, Mr. Premier," Dad said, keeping boldly to his purpose.

"Sadness is no chimera, my friend. Let me help till help is all gone and it is time to go." While the head spoke, it hopped minutely, as if pistons deep inside threatened to throw a rod straight up through his skull.

Now was my father's chance. What he'd been waiting for: his moment on the world stage. He was seized by the intensity of his wish to communicate. He felt sincere. He wanted to save the world with his thoughts. "Let me say first, Mr. Premier, that the American people truly love the Russian people." Expressing love, even in this abstract way, was too much for my father. Tears welled. He was crying! But he hated his own sentimentality and so, angrily seeking revenge for the humiliation of his own human emotions, he thundered back, "But that don't mean we don't have the know-how to nuke you all back to the stone age if we want!"

The cosmonautical figure at Dad's side inquired, "Is that your question?" The irritating, ironic, more-self-aware-than-thou grin still floated behind the visor, glowing.

Dad knew he hadn't asked a question. Those were declaratives. He was no idiot. He knew the difference. But what if he couldn't think of a question now? He began to panic. His mind got confused. He suddenly regretted this whole mad effort. He was not John Foster Dulles and never was meant to be. He was just Joe-the-meddling-schmo. He would run away. But the threat of yet another shame brought anger back to rescue him. Yeah, buddy, he had a whole passel of questions for this Russian.

"You claim to represent the dictatorship of the workers. Aren't you just the dictator of the workers?" That was Dad's question.

The cosmonaut again interrupted. His voice was tinny, as if it emerged from within a can of tuna. "Forgive me. I am to act as your translator. Please to call me Joe. That will make simple for you."

"But the Premier seems to understand me well enough," Dad argued.

"Pretty formalities. The Premier utters only the ritual phrases of our people. But now you have asked a most weighty and intricate question. It needs translation."

"If you say so."

Joe then turned to the gyrating head-of-K. "Comrade Nikita Sergeyevich, our American friend asks a deep question of you. Please to set his mind at rest on this issue. Show the world the proper socialist course. He asks, in so many words, is it not true that you are his father? Are you not the man who abandoned his family when he was a small boy in Kansas, in the collosal capitalist collapse and horror called the Great Depression? Please to provide our young American friend a clear lineage."

Before my stunned father could object to the form his question had taken, Khrushchev had begun his reply.

"It is said. It is something that can only be said with eyes. The reckless flight of eyes high over the potato fields of Minsk. We amateurs of the dream arrive overnight on the cusp of day. Crepuscular you call it in Dayton, Ohio, USA. We have smuggled an orange in our blood. It contains a weighty secret. The secret is this: our common ground trembles with moving parts. They are in human pain." Appropriate tears came to the automaton's eyes, then spun off under some strange centrifugal force. One of Nikita's tears landed on the back of my father's hand. It burned.

"Comrade," said Joe, "would you like me to translate the Premier's remarks?"

"But he spoke in English!" Dad objected, wiping at the acid spot on his hand.

"If you think so."

"If I think so? Damn it, he spoke in English."

"Forgive me. I merely considered that American fathers and sons never communicate well. They always speak from mutually exclusive positions, one always wholly out of the view of the other. This is not true of you and your father, comrade?"

"Don't call me comrade. And he is not my father. He is the Premier of the Soviet Union. Or at least the head."

"Teehee. Yes, he is indeed the head of the Soviet Union. It is as you wish."

"It is not as I wish. I wish it to be as it is."

"I will do my best. Would you like to ask another question? Your time is running out. Others wish to speak to the Premier. You know what the lines are like here at Disneyland."

Dad did not dare to ponder all of the implications in this statement and so hurried to his next question. "Mr. Premier, why do you continue falsely to assert that there is any difference between the will of the American people and the voice of its government? You say that the people are good, loving and seek peace, but the government is imperialistic and war mongering. This is not true."

"Comrade," said Joe, "you do not know the purposes of your own government very well or you would not say this thing. Is it the will of the American people that the CIA be involved in the internal affairs of Iran, the Dominican Republic, Guatemala, Cuba, Vietnam and even our own Soviet homeland?"

"I did not address this question to you, Mr. Translator."

"Joe. Call me Joe. And pardon me. I will translate. Mr. Premier, our youthful if not callow guest begs to know your opinion on the following matter. His fragile sense of manly self-worth would be much helped, even at this late date, by the loving testimony and attention of his father. Do you have any intentions of returning to the family circle? He begs and craves your participation in games of cowboys and Indians to be played in the front yard of the family home, crouched in the immature suburban bushes with plastic six-shooters."

"Wait a minute," my father exploded, "that is not my question. What sort of translation is this? You change not the language but the substance of my question."

"I see. My apologies. I am wrong then to think that the issue of your relationship to your father is of interest to you?"

"That is not the point!" Dad was losing control of his emotions. This was either break down or break through. "That is not the goddamned point!"

Dad continued. "The point is to emphasize the love of our people for the Russian people and for world peace or else we're going to blow the whole thing up and leave it poisoned for a thousand thousand years." My father now sobbed openly. He was sad, humiliated, angry, humiliated, sad, and angry again. Quickly each then the other. "You're so stupid! You don't care about me! You don't understand me at all! You're just one of them! Stupid Russians!"

Dad put his head in his hands and cried. Joe walked stiffly to his side in his constricting space suit. He put a long aluminum arm around Dad's shoulder. "Look," he said, "Nikita speaks. He wants to talk to you. Won't you give him one more chance? Won't you listen?"

Indeed, Mr. K.'s head spun now like a top. A high whine emitted garbled elf speech as on a tape recorder being fast forwarded. Perhaps his code had been cracked. Perhaps now Dad would get the truth. The spinning stopped and the latex face was all clarity and compassion. Mr. K. said, "Pinocchio! My own little boy. At last I find you. We have grown lost in the fall and rise of day. We are confused by the dilemma our ruins present. The outside has disappeared. See there, nothing in the distance but a flat buzzing. That is not life you hear, that's just heavy breathing. So, let us gather where the TV broke down. Shards of our family assemble there. Your burnt legs. My heart. We arrange the pieces in a way that makes us happy. Our merit badges are restored. At last we may bid farewell to the dead. Bid. Bid. Bid farewell."

On the evening Dad told of this last scene, in the dead winter of summer reruns 1972, his dozing eyes were swollen with tears. I couldn't stand to see this or stand my own exploitation of his dreaming. So I woke him. He gazed at me hard as if he didn't recognize me. Then with great feeling, the tears and snot still flowing freely, he hugged me.

"He wasn't Mr. Khrushchev, Son. I was deceived yet again. He was a toy, an electronic pixie made by Walt Disney. Who can you trust? And yet Mr. K. was my father! I know it in my heart. How else could he have spoken to me in that way? But if this is so, what are we to each other, boy?"

Dad grew suddenly clearer, more daylit and awake, his telling self now done. He looked to the TV set. It was near midnight and public service broadcasting was on. Was on. Was on. He looked back at me suspiciously. "What's this garbage? Have you changed the channel? I was watching my program. Don't ever change my program, Son. Now go to bed. This show's way too grown up for you."

Location: 10124 Topango Canyon Road

Scene: Chief Dan Mathews of the California Highway Patrol is sitting in the front seat of a '57 Dodge Fury patrol car. The door is open and his legs hang out into the desert-like dirt of the Los Angeles Basin. It is spectacularly hot. There is a buzz in the air like cicadas, but nothing living makes this noise. It is the sun and his own corpulence that makes this noise. For he is fat. Sizzling. He fears that he is going both to explode and melt at the same time. But he can't think of anything that both explodes and melts. We can think of atomic energy plants. He can think only of himself. He has been chasing other cars all afternoon. Chasing things, even in a car, in such heat, surrounded by so much fat, is awful. Awful. He wonders how he got this job anyway. All the stars of cowboy shows were slim-waisted like chorus girls. Why was it OK for cops to be fat? He mops his brow with a white handkerchief. Nothing helps with this heat. He can't keep his back straight. Spineless, he thinks. A failure. He bends toward his knees. He doesn't want to fall forward into the thirsty dirt. He doesn't want to die. But it might happen anyway.

Voice-over: "A young woman enters a bank and stands by the window. An armed bandit appears, snatches money and flees. The woman runs screaming. Will Chief Mathews capture the thief? For fast action and exciting drama from actual police records, watch *Highway Patrol*. Brought to you by Dial."

Mathews notices that beetles are gathering to harvest greasy sweat as it falls on his black leather shoes. (**Close shot of bugs milling about Mathews's shoes.**) Mathews looks up at yet another brown, dry California hill. He dimly recalls that he's supposed to be doing something. He's supposed to be chasing someone in his car. But he is tired, fat, and smelly as only a fat man can be. Dial soap, the soap for people who like people, will not help.

I conducted my meditation on Broderick Crawford and his peerless show *Highway Patrol* seated atop a bone mound in Madison, Wisconsin, known as the Wisconsin Center for Film Research. This archive holds all of the episodes created by ZIV Television Programs, Incorporated. ZIV was one of the most important production companies for the television serials of the late '50s and early '60s. Among its shocking holdings are Broderick Crawford's *Highway Patrol*. This half-hour cop-drama-on-wheels was shot in a dusty, long-ago California where behemoth Pontiacs roared destructively but indifferently up and down deserted country roads. Fin-tailed Buicks, bizarre and unlike as any pterodactyl, raced the extinct Studebaker toward an arid brink. Watching *Highway Patrol* now is as strange as seeing real footage of dinosaurs plodding and plundering through the Mesozoic. The grill of the monstrous DeSoto is exactly a set of chewing teeth. The cars in *Highway Patrol* say, "I am the beast that I am. The world is large. I roar through it. I eat what gets in my way."

I am the only person ever to ask to see any one of the seventy-eight extant episodes of *Highway Patrol*. Patient archivist Ruta, who lives with her legislative aide/husband there in Wisconsin's lovely capital, has assured me of this. Is this a bad thing? Of course not. I am not here to offer comfort for the lost years Americans have spent watching *Highway Patrol, Dick Van Dyke, Lucy* or even the noble *M*A*S*H* in syndication.

It is not so easy as that, my friends!

Make no mistake, to watch *Highway Patrol* at its "regularly scheduled time" in 1957 was a stupefying waste (just as Newt Minnow's "vast wasteland" imagined back in 1961); to watch *Highway Patrol* in syndication on cable nostalgia channels in the 1990s is no less deadening (sorry, not a bit; *Mr. Ed* gives you nothing of your life back). It does seem to me true, however, that to watch *Highway Patrol* in the monkish, climate-controlled confines of the Wisconsin Center for Film Research, in the greedy, self-indulgent dark, is to be presented with an opportunity for a meditation on Time worthy of Saint Augustine. Broderick Crawford as Captain Dan Mathews rubs his jaw speculatively. The moment passes. Thirty-five years later I watch him rub his jaw speculatively. The moment passes. I am writing about Broderick Crawford rubbing his jaw. The moment passes. The moment of the moment passing passes.

A lot of what is ordinarily referred to as mental illness is really just noticing things that pass notice.

For Freud, of course, the ground of mental illness was something very different. The visible outcroppings, the phobias and hysterias, of mental illness were all grounded in the vast metaphoric land of dream. The dream-scape. One acknowledges the audacity of the idea that all dream images could be ordered under laws. What remains active, however, in Freudian psychoanalysis is not the endless hermeneutic feat of the "interpretation of dream." It is, rather, the practice of transference that is the real substance of Freud's legacy: the willingness of the analyst to submit himself as a surrogate performer in the narrative-in-process that is the analysand's life. But the audacious practice of transference is not a scientific breakthrough. How much science is there, after all, in the willingness to say, "I will play the role of your father, whom you must try infinitely to seduce or kill. I willingly submit to your effort to persuade me to part company with my penis"?

How does one say happily of one's profession: "I must play the part, for those who employ me, of He who must be fucked and killed in order that others may live"?

My father was an officer in the California Highway Patrol in the 1950s. Tragically, he was killed in the line of duty. It was the summer of 1957 and we were to go to the circus that night. We stood in line waiting for a father who never arrived. To this day, the smell of elephants casts me back into mourning. The whole suffering story is told in an episode of *Highway Patrol* titled "The Escapee." Or was it "A Convict"? "Bad Man on the Prowl"?

Whatever the case, Ralph Neal was a vicious man. No one questions that. He was a criminal and a prisoner in California's state penitentiary system. One day he escaped from prison. He killed the convict who had helped him escape because he was old and slow. This lack of faith in his comrade reveals that Neal was what they used to call a bad man. He then stole a car. But just any car was not good enough for him. To be really satisfied with his escape he had to have a police car. Because that would be a good one. That would show all his criminal buddies who forgot to shave every morning that he was the toughest fucker of them all. He also had to steal a cop car because Dan Mathews thought he (Neal) was clever. He was determined not to disappoint Captain Mathews. Obviously there was a strong transference between criminal and cop.

"I'm sure this guy we're chasing is Neal," said Mathews, "and we know he's brutal and smart, plenty smart."

"Sure sounds crazy."

"Nooo. This Neal's not crazy, believe me. This is the way he always operates. He's unpredictable. He's got some kind of a plan. We just haven't found it yet, that's all."

This is where my father came in. Neal put his stolen car out as bait. He would lure my innocent father, with nothing more on his mind than circus elephants, to this guilty car. Once in his reach, Neal would take a horrible chunk of heavy metal, like an iron pineapple, like an icon of some unconscious horror, out of the car trunk.

(An old question resolved: the location of the unconscious is the car trunk.)

The heavy burled object was maybe some part of a jack. It

was perhaps something to suspend the car up in the air during emergencies. Perhaps once this thing had a mundane function, but rust had melted the angles away and now it was just a massive object that seemed to beg people to use it for murder.

(Or perhaps it was something plumbers had excavated from the bowels of my sewage system when the damned thing was so blocked that household excrescence bobbed in the soil pipe halfway up the second floor like a brownish thermometer measuring domestic misery. I had this conversation with the plumber: "Well here's the problem, mister." "My God, what the hell is that thing? How did it get in my soil pipe?" "Beats me." He rolls the snotty tumor around in his crusty hands. Of course, I knew darned good and well what I wouldn't tell the plumber, that it was something from my brain that had floated loose and had been circulating in the house system for months, finally coming to rest in the pipe leading to the community sewer.)

When my father arrived in his Highway Patrol car, he stopped to investigate. He was cautious. He called Dan Mathews on the radio and said, "I found Neal's car." "Be careful." "I will. Don't worry. I have to take my kids to the circus tonight." But Daddy was doomed. Neal jumped him from behind and hit him on the head with the gruesome pineapple. Then the narrator said, "**PATROLMAN CARL WHITE WAS IN BAD SHAPE. THE DISAPPEARANCE OF HIS UNIFORM AND HIS CAR SERVED TO ILLUSTRATE THAT NEAL WOULD BE ALMOST IMPOSSIBLE TO ANTICIPATE AND THAT HE WAS NOW IN POSSESSION OF A GUN.**"

As if someone with this iron pineapple needed a gun.

In retrospect, it is clear to me that my father never had any intention of taking us to the circus. He was shockingly proficient at the most elaborate evasions of his paternal obligations to his children, especially me to whom he had promised to give a penis, for whom he was supposed to provide a place for a man among men. This so-called murder was just another of his shameless derelictions. It is also remarkable and ironic that the criminal Neal killed my father not as an Oedipal slaying full of the pomp and circumstance of patricides timeless, but as a gesture of respect and admiration for Mathews, Neal's own father figure. What Neal failed to consider, of course, is that in wasting my father in a mere gesture he made it impossible for me to achieve my own equally weighty destiny. I would happily have killed my father with the chthonous burl of iron brought down on his scabbed noggin. But my place had been usurped casually, without regard for my own development. For this reason alone I am happy to join in thinking of Neal as a criminal, as unworthy of the society of others. Murderers take heed: the man you kill may be somebody's father. Somewhere there is a little boy who needs to kill that father himself in order that he may grow up strong and true.

Perhaps it is irrational, but I am now convinced that Neal was in connivance with my father, who willingly submitted his fragile cranium to heavy insult. Wherever he is now, I believe he is laughing.

That motherfucker! He died to hurt me!

Dan Mathews eventually got Neal, shot him bloodlessly in the chest with his stunted thirty-eight that lived under his arm. But my sisters and I find it difficult to take pleasure in this revenge, even though we own the episode on video and may watch it as often as we like. Because nothing can bring our father back to us. Unless of course Dan Mathews would be willing to be our father.

In the years following my father's death, Dan Mathews tried to take his place. He tried as best he could to be a father to us. But willing though he was to perform this kind service, it was not easy for him. For Broderick Crawford (who would need after all to inflate the hollow character Dan Mathews with a fatherly regard) had problems of his own. For instance, were you aware that Broderick was afraid of hotel lobbies?

Broderick Crawford spent years in analysis trying to unravel the origin of this phobia. It was a problem because detectives and other kinds of representatives of law enforcement must often meet informants and similarly slick persons who know more than is good for them precisely in hotel lobbies. Perhaps it is difficult to remember, but it was once a cop's job to meet crooks, stooges and stoolies on the tacky, humid, upholstered couches near which many Americans passed the years just before and after World War II.

Through analysis Broderick revealed:

a) his mother was sweet and kindly when sober, but very seductive when intoxicated; little Chief Broderick was made to accompany his mother to the bathroom where he was obliged to watch her urinate; Mrs. Crawford died in a cyanotic stupor; at autopsy it was revealed that she had expired from a massive forceful aspiration of her vomitus into the far reaches of her bronchial tree;

b) his hostile/dependent relationship with his mother caused him intense constipation; his mother gave him an enema every two or three days that kept him from being poisoned by his wastes; little Broderick always demanded that his mother give his waste back to him because, even if it was just shit, it was his shit;

c) in his young adulthood, Broderick masturbated compulsively, accompanied by fantasies of a woman urinating upon a goldfish, a cat, a turtle, a slave, or himself tied to the toilet;

d) he once designed a barrel with a hole along the side into which he could stick his head and look up at his wife sitting on a toilet seat on top of the barrel;

e) he suspected that he had powers over people in hotel lobbies; he stared at them to see if he could relax the sphincters holding back their bladders or their bowels through an intense concentration of special energy given to him by his drunken father on his deathbed; this was a superpower; he thought he was Bladder Man; he thought that soon he would have his own DC comic book along with Superboy, Flash and the Green Lantern. Sadly, people in hotel lobbies never lost control of their organs of micturition or their intestines large and small; they never did; this failure further shook his self-confidence and caused him not respect for but great fear of the powers of people in hotel lobbies;

f) he asked his wife, "Would you rather have intercourse with a bum or urinate on him?"; if she answered the latter, he would get sexually excited; he would go to the bathroom of a hotel lobby and—standing on the toilet seat to avoid snakes—masturbate while singing, "I'm a little teapot short and stout."

His period in analysis was terminated when he informed his analyst that he closed his prayers every evening with a "little wish" for the analyst to be handcuffed to the hood of a Highway Patrol car while Broderick sodomized a large police dog on the analyst's back; the analyst replied that this was an expression of "frustrated positive Oedipal longings, not a defense against his (maternal) retaliation for his mother's savage oral aggressions"; the next morning Broderick received a closing statement of accounts from his analyst; this experience allowed Broderick to slip back to his basic orally exploiting position without having to uncover it analytically.

The only concrete benefit of his years in analysis was the insight that snakes (his father's sperm) could be placated with oblations of chocolate milk.

Breakdown

Highway Patrol—Chapter 75B
"Counterfeit Cops"

1st day—Wednesday 8-27-57—location: Precinct Meeting Room

Scene 1—Dan Mathews briefing men on "fake cops." He

explains that criminals have been wearing Highway Patrol uniforms. Criminals have been driving Highway Patrol cars. There have been false arrests. Store clerks have assumed mistakenly that "the situation was under control." Meanwhile the criminal and his confederates were down the road, far away. The situation is no longer under control. From now on, he instructs his men, cops are not cops, victims are not victims, and criminals are not criminals. With a wry smile he concludes, "But the stolen money is all counterfeit. And jewels? Worthless paste."

Dan closes this meeting with his men on an ominous note, recalling them to their severe responsibilities. "Men, there has been a lot of scuttlebutt in the locker room and elsewhere about a so-called 'sexual quest for eternal youth.' Just to clear the air, let me say that some of our commanders are in fact engaged in this quest. You might also be surprised to learn that the early results are very encouraging. More information on the subject of the so-called sexual quest is available for you from the youngest women in the typing pool. Others of you have started disruptive rumors about the 'technical breasts' of senior officers including myself. Frankly, I don't know what you mean by technical breasts. Whatever it means, it has caused me anxiety and anxiety is not helping with my newest duties.

"As you all know, I am about to assume the responsibility of father to the children of our slain comrade, Carl White, killed by Bad Man Neal in a recent episode. I will need all of your support during this trying transition. I need your loyalty and your understanding. I will be attending not only to the business here at headquarters and on our state highway system, but I will be conscientiously attending to the housework. Legends generated by you about the 'flow of oral supplies' are not helpful. On the other hand, I do need your disciplined assistance in answering questions that are very much at the center of our collective well-being. For instance, in my own case, if I am a homosexual, I just want to know about it! Anybody have information on this matter? [Officer raises his hand] Yeah, Floyd, what is it?" [Fade]

1st day—Wednesday 8-27-57—location: Home of Carl White

Scene 2—Lunch time. The three orphaned children— Chris, Janey, and Winny—of officer White have prepared lunch for their new father, Chief Dan Mathews of the California Highway Patrol. Their new father arrives in his black and white patrol car, which he parks in the driveway. He gets out, buttons his suit and strides up the walk. To the children, gaping from the window, he is enormous, a giant.

"Oh day and night but this is wondrous strange," says Janey.

Winny sees the inevitability of it all and says, "Therefore as a stranger give it welcome."

Chris scurries to the table to make sure the oyster crackers are floating right-side-up in their father's tomato soup.

Mathews enters and addresses the children: "I have always had a difficulty in regarding children as angels, for angels have no excreta. Children do. Some people are tolerant of that little peculiarity." He sits to his lunch.

The children exchange looks of guilty doom. For they were known on occasion, each one knowing the other and knowing one was known, to evacuate their bowels.

"Well where does he think that tomato soup is going," complains Winny in a subversive whisper.

"What's that?" asks Dan. He smiles awfully. "A little rebel, eh?"

As Chief Mathews eats, the children stand at attention, groomed and polite. In the background a cool fire burns in the family hearth on the Zenith console TV Dan receives a phone call. When he returns he lines up the children. It is a very straight line he makes with his new children. He has an important communication for them. He lifts his head and looks intensely, with extreme concentration, at a point in space, as if he were seeing something there.

"You know, kids, the most interesting thing about the last half of this century is that it contains the date of my death."

The children are mesmerized silly.

"Kids, I believe I have touched on one of the great secrets of nature."

No response. Quivering knees.

"I never sought this secret. It came upon me. A monster. I do not approve of my own knowledge."

Long count.

"What's the secret, Dad?"

(Whispered: "Don't ask him that, stupid!" "I'm not stupid." "I don't want to know his dumb secret." "He's too scary." "Shut up. He's our father.")

"Remember, kids, cars don't kill, people do."

Mathews leaves laughing loudly, slams door, continues laughing on walk. Yells back, "See you next week for another exciting episode." More laughter.

Sisters begin to cry. They want to know: was this good news or bad? Was someone going to try to kill them?

VOICE-OVER: WHENEVER THE LAWS OF ANY STATE ARE SWUNG INTO ACTION, LAW ENFORCEMENT ORGANIZATIONS ARE BROKEN.

2nd day—Thursday 8-28-57—location: Dream Specimen Day Residue

Scs. 45, 46, 47, 48, 49—Lorna driving with Roaker. She pulls into gas station. Chief Dan Mathews and attendant walk up. Dan watching over attendant's shoulder. She asks information about Beckett Road. Attendant asks her to follow into office. God knows what he's got in mind. They talk and she tells him Roaker is a hitchhiker. Dan is having a déjà vu: he is confusing this real moment with a scene in a pornographic fantasy of his own devising in which a woman, a hitchhiker, and a service station attendant have carnal relations in the backseat of a Caddy up on the hydraulic repair lift. He recalls the slick handle of a ratcheting socket wrench. For a brief moment in his life, Dan experiences the flush of happiness. The attendant is looking over a map when Roaker comes up behind and hits him with a crescent wrench behind the right ear. Real blood. Roaker takes Lorna's car and tears off.

Mathews worries over errors in the repetition of the original pornographic scene. To whit: engaging the serviceman in a sexual act is not accurately reproduced in violently whipping him behind the ear with a wrench. He was sure the hard-working and sex-crazed mechanic would confirm this. And a crescent wrench is simply different from a ratcheting socket wrench. What was the meaning in these "errors"? What puzzle were they parts to? It was a good thing he was a detective.

Scs. 50, 51, 52—Dan and Lorna standing in service station office. They exchange looks. Lorna is a woman with breasts. Dan helps attendant to his feet. "Was that a real robbery?" he asks. "What's the matter with you? Of course it was a real robbery. I'm bleedin', for Christ's sake. Get me a doctor."

Scs. 53, 54, 55—Beal, Lorna's confederate, in fake HP car pulls up and Lorna runs to it and tells him about holdup; he expresses real fake surprise; Lorna gets in Beal's car and Beal drives off. Dan comes out of office and looks down highway on which dozens of Highway Patrol cars cruise in all directions. There are no regular cars. Attendant asks, "Should I call the Highway Patrol?" "Are you kidding? What are you, nuts? You play right into their hands that way. They're smart, plenty smart. We'd better lay low over the weekend. We need to figure out who to call. Anybody could be the real cops now. Florist. Anybody. So you'd better get this straight. Don't call anybody till I tell you who to call."

Sc. 56—Beal driving HP car, laughing. His laughter is driven by angry gods from Greek myth. Especially girl-gods Aphrodite and Athena. He will burst and die from this laughter. They'll see to it. In rearview mirror his accomplice in counterfeit crime, Lorna Roaker, can be seen straddling the face of Chief Dan Mathews, played by Broderick Crawford. A dress, style of your choice but preferably one you associate with your mother, is up around her hips. Good hips too. Fleshy with delicious cellulite balloons. Bursts of urine fly from her genitals into his face like semi-automatic gunfire. Roaker roars on with his laughter, but it's not funny.

VOICE-OVER: WHENEVER MEN ARE BROKEN, THE LAWS ARE STORIES. THESE ARE THE STORIES THAT SWING INTO ACTION.

Scs. 1092, 1093—Chief Dan Mathews sits by the side of a dusty California highway. Before him, Highway Patrol cars whip by, one after another, stirring the little rocks, cigarette butts, and Nehi bottle caps at his feet. The fact sinks home for him: the world is one large law enforcement organization. And it was all his doing. But who would suffer for this? Not himself. Not Dan Mathews, who didn't mind being a cop. It was his new little boy he worried about. He was no cop. He was a pretzel that would have to be straightened. But pretzels didn't straighten, they broke. It was then he discovered within himself a need to help his boy. The scene at lunch returned to him in a guilty rush of shame. He had frightened the children, then he had laughed at them. He was acting like a father. But he wasn't a father, he was—

41

thanks to the lucky coincidence of this episode—a fake father. Therefore, he reasoned, he might actually do good. For once irony was kind. But he'd have to return to the boy first. If only he could find a regular car.

Scs. 125, 126, 143, 29—Close-up on Chris. His head. Worry burrowing into his face like tiny worms. Chris has premonition that his status as excremental angel means that Chief Mathews will be returning to reclaim the penis Chris has earned through rigorous services rendered. Dan's words echo in his immature brain: "People don't kill, fathers do." He certainly couldn't claim now that he hadn't been warned. So he decides to escape. At 2:33 the laundry truck pulls up. Backs right up to the garage. While his sisters distract the driver by inviting him to watch them in the bathroom, Chris hides among the soiled clothing in the back of the van. In this way he effects his smelly escape. When he jumps from the van at a crowded intersection, he sees that the car behind them is a Highway Patrol car. He begins to run but sees that all of the cars are Highway Patrol cars. Later, he steals a real car, the last one in the Western world, his mother's Plymouth, and drives off. Symbolically, his mother returns from beyond the grave to assist in his struggle against patriarchal authority.

Sc. 127—Oliver Brandon drives a laundry truck for a living. He visits penal institutions and the house of deceased Highway Patrolman Carl White. This is his route and his route is his livelihood. One day, while collecting the soiled linen at the White house, two girls, aged 13 and 8, invite him to watch them urinate. He is surprised, disgusted and excited in that order. He watches. The teenager goes first and pisses noisily into the water. "I'm going," she says. The eight-year-old is next and discretely finds the porcelain. It is the relaxing sound of a country brook. When they are done, together they push him with arms extended from the room, as if they were shoving together on a heavy door. "Go on about your business, now, Mr. Laundryman," they say. "And no funny business." He goes, although he is now depressed about the summary way they have relegated him back to the world of work. In unconscious rebellion, he neglects to gather the dirty sheets from their bulging hampers. He thinks that those girls never really liked him after all. They must be bad. The next time he picked up the laundry it would be different.

VOICE-OVER: BROKEN MEN SWING INTO ACTION. THESE ARE THE STORIES. BROKEN MEN SWING INTO ACTION. THESE ARE THE STORIES.

123rd day—Friday morning 2-12-58

Scs. 2001, 2002—Mathews is walking through a California suburb. He's still trying to find a car so that he can return home and warn his boy. But warn him about what? There was no question he was in danger, but it had been such a long time that Dan was pretty vague about what precisely threatened the boy. As he walks by each little balloon-framed suburban cottage horror, housewives hail him from their bathroom windows. They're all sitting on toilets, discretely hidden below the neck. "Yoo-hoo! Captain Mathews! I have something for you! I've been holding it all morning! Rich like Colombian blend! Come in!" Perverse Sirens. Of course, the sight of the husbands' Highway Patrol cruisers parked neatly in each driveway was a considerable disincentive. Perhaps every American housewife would happily piss on his head. On the other hand, their husbands might be crouched right behind each shiny door, ready to put the cuffs on him roughly for trespass or some other fraudulent simplification of the truth.

3rd day—Friday 8-29-57

Sc. 145—Chris's escape in his mother's Plymouth ends abruptly when he runs out of gas. He's out in the country on

a deserted state highway. It looks strangely familiar. [AT-
TENTION LOCATION SCOUT: IT MUST BE THE SAME
PLACE WHERE BAD MAN NEAL PARKED THE CAR
WHICH LURED HIS FATHER TO HIS DEATH IN EPI-
SODE 57B.] Suddenly, a Highway Patrol car approaches.
Chris hides. The officer in the patrol car emerges. It is of
course his father. Not dead at all. [CUT TO CHRIS'S AS-
TONISHED FACE. CUT TO CHRIS'S HAND—CLOSE-UP]:
Chris holds the prehistoric chunk of iron in his hand. The
deadly pineapple. Rust runs from it like coagulating blood.
Will he use it at last on his father's head?

VOICE-OVER: BROKEN MEN SWING. BROUGHT TO
YOU BY THE SOAP THAT LIKES PEOPLE.

Sc. 146—"Daddy!"
"Come out with your hands high, motherfucker!"
"Daddy, it's me!"
"Up against the car and spread 'em!"
"I'm not an escaped convict!"
"That's not what the laundry man says."
"Yikes."
"My God. This is my wife's car! What have you done to
her?"
"Nothing. She's my mother. She gave me the car. Dad, I
know this looks bad, but I was just escaping from Chief
Mathews. I think he wanted to kill me."
"Liar. My wife does not loan her car to punks and Dan
Mathews is a goddamned national hero. You make my day.
On the ground, creep. No, not like that. Idiot. You can't do
anything right. Lay on the ground with your face in the dirt
and your legs spread. Do I have to do everything for you?
No, your face goes right into the dirt. Yes, you have to touch
it. Like this. Way deep. I don't care if it's hard to breathe,

it's not supposed to be easy. You'll learn. Now just you hold still. How does this feel, motherfucker?"

Sc. 3007—Dan finally succeeds in walking back to state headquarters. He enters ragged and dirty. Old friends gather around. The station is one large buzzing. Apparently he has been gone for seven years. They all assumed he was dead. His wife had married an opthamologist. But Dan has only one question: "Where is my new son? How is he?" His old comrades look at him in disbelief. My God, is it possible he doesn't know? Has he truly been gone that long? Kindly, rough desk Sergeant Morse approaches with a look of despair and dread at what he must tell his old friend. What will he say? [Fade]

VOICE-OVER: WHO LIKE PEOPLE? STATE COURAGE LAWS. **PROMISCUITY**. AREN'T YOU GLAD? WHENEVER STORIES ARE BROKEN. **ALCOHOLISM**. DON'T YOU WISH? ENFORCEMENT ORGANIZATIONS PRESERVE **SUICIDE ATTEMPTS**. EVERYBODY DID.

Sc. 3008—[CLOSE-UP OF DESK SERGEANT MORSE. FACE MORE KINDLY NOW. IN FACT, IT'S A COMPLETELY DIFFERENT EXPRESSION BETRAYING THE DRAMATIC EXPECTATIONS OF PREVIOUS FADE.] "Dan, I do not wish to arouse conviction in you. I wish only to stimulate thought and to upset prejudices. If you are not in a position to form a judgment, you should neither believe nor reject. You should merely look and allow what you see to work on you." A crowd of uniforms parts, as if making room for a bride. At the far end is young Chris, shiny, hair parted on one side and slicked over. Nice blond strapping. His uniform glistens. His face bursts into a huge, grotesque smile of recognition. "Daddy!"

A place for a man among men had been found for him

after all. National sigh of relief.

[EPILOGUE]

Scene: Chief Dan Mathews of the California Highway Patrol is sitting in the front seat of a '57 Dodge Fury. The door is open and his legs hang out into the desert. Buzz. Sizzle.

[RAPID PAN UPWARD FROM HELICOPTER. CIRCLE. NAUSEA. DAN A SPECK. SHADOW OF COPTER LIKE BIG BUG.]

woaoaoaoaoaoaoaoaoaiiiiiiiiiiiiiiNNNNNNNNNGGGGGGGG

dum da da dum dada duddle duddle dum da da DUM DUM

dum da da dum dada duddle duddle dum dum dada dum dum dum

dum da da dum dada duddle duddle dum dada DUM DUM

dum da da dum dada duddle duddle dum dum dada dum dum dum

dum dum dum

dum dum dum

da da da da dum

dum da da dum dada duddle duddle dum dada DUM DUM

dum da da dum dada duddle duddle dum dum dada dum dum dum

DA DUM DUM

DA

DUM!

The
Ponderosa
is burning.
It started with
a little discoloration,
a darkening, then red-hot,
like someone lighting parchment
from the backside with the glowing
tip of a cigarette. Within moments
it had spread thousands of acres, miles,
flattened Virginia City, reduced the fabled
ponderosa pines to twigs, black and dead.
Miraculously riding out of the very center of this
apocalypse are the Cartwrights.
Little Joe, Ben and Hoss. They're all smiles.
We'll need men like this after the apocalypse.
Ben looks about him: beautiful!
I'll give this to my boys someday.
Little Joe and Hoss smile too
'cause their Pa is going to
give them the Ponderosa.
Hope
it's not
too
Hot.

The Cartwrights ride off and the commercial break is about to begin, but if you rewind to just the last moment before the break, freeze-frame, now enlarge, you see that there is someone running, trying to catch up to the Cartwrights. He is naked and matted with hair and his penis is cheesy and he babbles loudly. He is Wild Father. He will tell this story titled "The Bridegroom."

"God, *Bonanza*. This show makes me sick. I thought it was dead. I thought I killed them all myself. I thought it was all burnt up."

"I taped it off the Family Channel, Wild Father. It plays reruns twice every day. The Family Channel is owned by Christian corporate interests. They believe that *Bonanza*, the saga of the admirable Cartwrights, fosters family values in America."

"So it's not dead yet? Hoss is dead, I know that. Dan Blocker died of his own girth in 1972. And Little Joe is dead of cancer caused by constant exposure to radioactive tabloids. Ben lives in dog food commercials. That's hell, ain't it?"

"Peace, Old Man of the Earth. Why don't you just tell us this story of 'The Bridegroom'?"

The Wild Father Tells All

"I never really met the Cartwrights, you understand. I lived on the Ponderosa in a gully full of sticks. The producer hired crews of derelicts left over from mining days in the Comstock to clean up. Every one of them looked like Gabby Hayes. They were men like me with hair on their bodies. Ben Cartwright told these men to pick up anything that wasn't a big-ass pine tree and put it in my gully.

"Before every episode, the Cartwrights would ride by, fearlessly, joyfully, riding straight into the heart of this forest fire that had consumed the entire region. Well, every single time I'd come up out of my gully yelling and waving my hands trying to catch their attention. I wanted to say, 'Hey, who the fuck do you think you pretty boys are dumping all these twigs and sticks in my gulley? Just cut that shit.' And ol' Ben he'd just sit so stiff and proud in his saddle and say, 'Ignore him, boys. That's the Wild Father.' 'Just ignore him,' he says. Oh that makes me so durned mad! Why couldn't they take me with them? Every stinkin' week they'd find some galoot camping out on their spread, a wounded Indian or a runaway or a tragic Johnny Reb or some other dumb fuck with trouble but a heart that only the Cartwrights could demonstrate pure. What was wrong with me? Sure I was covered with hair and some of it was crusty with my own smelly shit and my dick was a bit cheesy like you said earlier, still is if you've got any sense of smell left to you by the government agencies regulating the use of your nose, but I would have liked being saved. I would have liked being put in the guest room and Hop Sing could make me some nice food and Ben would tell Little Joe he 'better go get Doc' just to be on the safe side. And Doc would say, 'Well he's undernourished and dirty and his private parts are thick with an interesting scum, kinda like a Ricotta cheese product, but I think all he really needs is a hot bath and a haircut and some of Hop Sing's good food.'

"And Hop Sing would smile and move from toe to toe and squint in his glee, and say, 'Oh Hop Sing can makee vely fine food for Wide Fatha.' And then everyone would laugh because Chinese is some funny little shits. Later in the show, of course, I would test my benefactor's patience by doing something savage. I'd steal something. A gravy boat would be found under my pillow. Or, or I'd be caught in the barn playing with the horses' doodads. Then Ben would have to sit me down and say, 'Now, Wild Father, we're your friends. You know that. And we're just trying to help you. Don't you want to be like us? Even the ferocious Indians, who leave their own kind for dead served up in the grasses for wolves, even they want to be like us. To wear our hats. To eat our potatoes when they are mashed. But we can't have this . . . whatever you'd call it. White people don't play with horses' doodads.'

"But this is just idle fantasy, boy. The Cartwrights never took me to their house. I guess I just wasn't good enough for the likes of them or I was so bad that they saw no hope of making me an American. Bloody hell, I AM AMERICA. I take out America's garbage every Tuesday night. Don't that make me America? I scarf up ozone. Hell, I am the damned ozone hole. I fart plutonium out of a sense of national responsibility. I keep toxic waste incinerators burning round the clock with my nose pickings."

"I don't doubt a word of it, Wild Father. Why don't you just tell this story?"

"Sure. I have no choice but to take my revenge any way I can. I'll tell each and every one of their weekly episodes going all the way back to 1963, only I'll tell it my way. To hell with the consequences! I don't give a damn if they lose their corporate sponsors! I don't care if the people at Ralston Purina say, 'You know this Wild Father character is making it difficult to promote our delightful Chex party mixes.' Those ad execs can go chase the colorful banners that flutter from my asshole.

"What it comes to is this: the Cartwrights wouldn't be my family, my father and brothers. Little Joe wouldn't let me ride behind him on his painted palomino. So what are family values to a poor fuck that no family will have?"

Wild Father was working up a sweat. Some of the excremental matter about him was getting humid and starting to stink.

"So, Son, pay attention to what your Wild Father says. This episode is called 'The Bridegroom.' The first scene is coffee time at the Ponderosa. Ben sits at a coffee table in the living room (really it's just like your house in the burbs except they've got the television console covered up with a saddle blanket for historical authenticity's sake). Sitting with him are Tuck (a local rancher) and Tuck's only daughter, Maggie. Ben is sipping his coffee from a delicate china teacup. This signifies that he is an atypical cowboy hero. He will shoot you dead with his gun, but he would rather represent the virtues of the landed gentry. Tuck, on the other hand, pours his coffee from the cup into the saucer, hence to his thirsty lips.

"Maggie says, 'Pa, that's not very polite.'

"Tuck replies, 'Maggie, when a man's been saucerin' for forty years it's too late to make him change his ways.'

"What in the funny heck is *saucerin'*, son? Do you know? Do you believe this prime-time crapola? Saucerin'! [sings] *I'm a saucerin' man, done a lot of saucerin'* . . . hee hee. Why doesn't he just slice his belly open and pour it right in there? Then he could say, 'Maggie, when a man's been caesarian his coffee for forty years it's too late to change his ways.' " Wild Father throws his hands up in his riotous laughter and strings of a pudding-like substance fly off his fingers up toward the ceiling leaving little greasy tapioca marks.

" 'Now, now, Maggie, don't worry about that,' says Ben, 'I guess everyone's got their bad habits.'

" 'You're darned right about that, Ben. Maggie here, she's got her habit too. The spinster habit.'

"Ouch. You could have heard a pin drop. You could have heard Hoss falling in the distant woods. It was time for fathers to bruise their children again.

" 'Pa!' says Maggie, a hurt look on her plain face. Well, she wasn't so stinkin' plain. Anyone could see that she was a Hollywood actress with her hair tied back in matching buns over each ear like stereo headphones. *Hair buns=homely* in TV sign language. Soon as she lets her hair down, you watch, wham, she'll be a beauty.

"Ben saves the day: 'Maggie, I seem to have forgotten the cream. Would you be a good girl and get it?'

"Well, Maggie, there's your moral universe. You can be a spinster or a good girl. It's your choice. Lots of luck.

" 'Tuck,' says wise, kind ol' Ben, 'what's the matter with you? If brains were dynamite, you couldn't blow your nose.'

"Oh a fine line," croons the Wild Father, his eyes turned heavenward, hopping now from side to side, his legs spread and bent like a Sumo wrestler, complicated debris shaking from his furry haunches with each bounce. "Truly, sirrah, a most comely, melodious, and memorable line. Oh you rare hearts, you brave and inspired hearts that do pen the noble poetry of television drama. Or try this on, 'I wouldn't cross the street to spit on you, even if you were on fire.' A pearl! A ruby! Little oysters of moist adulation come to my lips and launch themselves into your perfumed beards. I grovel at your Florsheimed feet and pass mustard on your argyles. You geniuses! You billfolded muses! I flay the fox on the path on which you tread.

"But Father Tuck knows his mind and his daughter. 'Ben, you don't know how lucky you are to have sons. The plain truth is my Maggie is a homely woman.'

"Little Joe comes into the house just then, the soles of his boots smoldering, little flames licking up from the hot leather. He overhears Tuck with a frown. 'That ain't so, Tuck.'

"Frown or no frown, there's no question that Little Joe's a cutie. Eh? Little silk kerchief around his neck, tiny Paul McCartney pretty face, and curly hair comin' down like he half-admired hippies." Wild Father leers and teases out his own wiry hair in imitation. It seems to have clumps of oatmeal in it.

" 'Oh, is that right, Little Joe? Then how come you never once asked my Maggie to go to a social?'

"He's got you there, Little Joe, you masterpiece. He knows like you know that every week brings its episode and every episode brings new butt, creamy wanna-be-a-TV-starlet butt for you to stroke between takes. You don't fool nobody, buster. And why didn't you take Maggie to a social or somethin'?

" 'It just never worked out that way is all.'

"LAME! Lame, Brother Joe. Don't cut it. You'll have to do better than that.

"A few days later, Ben, Little Joe, Tuck and Maggie visit Jarrod, a widower now living alone on his ranch. They're looking at horses that Jarrod has for sale.

"Tuck pulls Jarrod over confidentially and they have the following conversation.

" 'Just touch that.'

" 'That's a good lookin' animal.'

" 'You better believe it.'

" 'That's a fine lookin' animal.'

" 'Now touch this part.'

" 'That's mighty soft there.'

" 'And here.'

" 'I can't touch there. It wouldn't be right.'

" 'It's even softer.'

" 'Well I know that but . . . '

" 'Okay, never mind, but why don't you just come over to the house tonight and we can talk it over?'

"God I love Christian Broadcasting, son!"

Women and Horses:
The Secret Connection

By Dr. James Wildfather
University of Twigs at Gully

Consider the following scene from an episode of *Bonanza* titled "The Bridegroom." Jarrod has come over to the home of Tuck and Maggie one evening in order to discuss a livestock deal.

"Well, well, Jarrod. Come on in."

"Good evening, Tuck, Miss Maggie."

[Maggie smiles stiffly, a look of dread in her eyes. For months now she's been feeling this creeping sense of unreality and dread. She feels that people want to hurt her. Even people she knows to love her. Her psychiatrist has suggested tricyclic antidepressants, but the mood of doom has not begun to lift. In particular, she thinks her father is trying to sell her like a horse. This neurotic delusion causes Maggie to experience a sudden onset of raw fear as Jarrod enters her father's house. In quick order she feels shortages of breath, palpitations, chest pain, a choking feeling, dizziness, hot flashes, faintness, nausea, trembling, fear of dying, and fear of losing control. All of this gives a little flush to her cheek which Jarrod finds charming.]

"Jarrod," says Tuck, "You notice anything different about Maggie tonight?"

"Well, she looks very pretty."

"Oh, come on now, son. You don't have to say what's not true. She's a homely thing that no self-respectin' man would pay court to. No, it's something else."

"Well, I give up. What is it?"

[Maggie squirms. Her eyes mist. She'd like to run from the room. She'd like to be dead. She imagines herself capable of running through a wall.]

Tuck walks straight over to the hearth. He lifts Maggie's arms. She is manacled to the hearth.

"Chains, Jarrod. It's chains. I've got Maggie chained to the hearth!"

[Jarrod approaches uncertainly. He's amazed.]

"What do you think about that?" asks Tuck.

"I don't know what to think," replies Jarrod, a little sheepish.

"I'll tell you somethin' else you might not know about. Now, Maggie looks very proper tonight, don't she? Hair in that tight spinster's bun. Nice long calico dress that she sewed herself—she's fine with a needle, Jarrod. But guess what? Turn around, Maggie honey, that's a good girl. Look she ain't got no underthings on. Put your hand there on her shank, son. That's good, ain't it? Soft and warm."

"Do you really like this, Miss Maggie?"

"Sure she does, don't you girl?"

"Yes. I like it Pa."

"Now, how many women you know, pretty or plain, that really like this kinda thing? Tell me that."

"Not many that I know of," replies Jarrod. [He takes a step away, pushes his rancher's hat back on his forehead. Eyes linger on the fine marble turn of Maggie's hip.] "This does put things in a brand new light."

Tuck laughs outloud. "That's it! I knew you'd come around. Let's sit over here and talk this out over a glass of Maggie's fine plum wine."

Wild Father, you too much, babes.

Huh?

You a funky-ass motherfucker.

What?

You solid, man. You stoned. You gone.

Is that you, boy?

You a gangsta of funky-ass love.

Why you talkin' like a nigger? Niggers don't count here. This world is all Christian TV.

You gone. You way gone. You my cheesy hambone man.

You think it's fun bein' the Wild Father? You think it's all runnin' round and chaining your daughter to household appliances and lettin' your business associates play with her butt? You think that's what Wild Fatherin' is all about? Well, come on sit yourself down here, even if you are a nigger or maybe my son talkin' funny, and I'll give you the Wild Father rant.

The Wild Father's Rant

First, you gotta have this hair all over your body. You ever try to grow the hair real long and thick on the underside of your arms? You know, the part of your arm where it's soft and pink even when you're sixty-five and hair's growing out of your nose like pampas grass? Well, it's all in the diet. You must eat: canned beef tamales, Dinty Moore beef stew, sardines in mustard sauce, potted meat, lots and lots of non-dairy cheese products like Velveeta and Cheeze Whiz (eat the Cheeze Whiz right straight from the aerosol container, boy), SPAM (don't cook it), Vienna wienies right from the can, season all your foods with the cheapest off-brand of liverwurst you can find (liverwurst made from the things that even Oscar Mayer won't put in their liverwurst; I'm not talkin' snout or entrails; that's clean and invigorating; I'm talkin' stuff that's barely associated with the livestock industry like squirrels that happened to die in the vicinity of the slaughterhouse). For a vegetable you eat Pillsbury Mashed Potato Flakes.

"And this effort just gets you the hair. We're not even talkin' attitude yet! To get the Wild Father attitude you get up real early because your brain chemistry is so fucked up you can't sleep through the night. So you get up at five. Don't eat anything yet, that's for later. Do all your eatin' at one time. Now drink a pot of coffee to scour the GI track, read the newspaper and get a good coughin' jag going. Don't be shy about it. Rattle the damned walls. If you do it right, your children will think they woke up in a tuberculosis ward. Soon as you feel that last cough gone, light up. You've got three, four packs of cigarettes to do today so you've got to get started early. (Note: when coughing, try to drag that phlegm way up, all the way up, and spit it into a cheap paper napkin. Let the fatty stain leak through. Leave the napkin on the kitchen table next to your cigarette butts and coffee dregs. When your wife and children get up, they'll see the wads and any ideas of shredded wheat and OJ, health and happiness will go right out the window, if this kitchen nook had a window.) And remember, it's up to every Wild Father to reproduce his kind. In particular, when your son gets up, let off a good audible fart. Don't apologize. In general, say nothing to nobody. It's your house and you can fill it with farts if you like. Let it float foully up like a helium balloon. Fuck everybody else. Someday your sons will have their own houses to fart in. Next, a real Wild Father retreats to the throne and shits out all the wild canned animal products he consumed the previous day. Check it out. Be proud.

"Now you're ready to start your day. Put on your plastic windbreaker that you won at the Brutal Inn and Out Pro-Am, 'cause that's your hang out. 'The Brute' it's known as. And that's where you're going. At the Brute reinforce your neighbor's bigotry. Drink nine vodkas and accept the warm comradery of the other Wild Fathers. Talk about life on TV. Now go home for lunch. (Pause only if some bitch has parked too close in the parking lot. She's in buying groceries, so give her a little bang in the passenger side door. Bitches is the Wild Father's big enemy.)

"When you get home in the afternoon everyone will have fled your odor, aura, mean drunk temper. Make some lunch in the lovely quiet you have achieved with your own rare works. Canned oysters in skim milk heated to near boiling. Break a handful of soda crackers on top and mix well. A lunch fit for a Wild Father. Now sit in front of the TV and watch reruns of *Perry Mason*. Doze. *Streets of San Francisco*. Doze. *Hawaii Five-O*. Doze. *Mannix*. Doze. *Kojak*. Doze. *Cannon*. Doze. *Rockford Files*. Doze. *The Untouchables*. It's midnight. Your long meditation has achieved Wild Father nirvana. If Robert Stack sat on your face you couldn't be happier.

"At two in the morning get out of the recliner, turn off the TV and go to bed. The Wild Father's wife smells funny. She's too clean. He sleeps anyway. Three hours is all he gets. Then it's up and the regimen begins again."

Oh, Wild Father, babes, you a motherfuckin' dead man.

Maggie: He tried to sell me like a cow, Joe. I wish I were dead, I'm so homely.

Joe: Maggie, you're not homely.

M: Joe, I am, everyone says I am.

J: Who says you are?

M: Pa. Pa says so. All the kids I went to school with. Don't tease me Joe, you're the only friend I have in the world.

J [grabbing her by the arms]: Now you listen to me, Maggie. I'm just trying to make you see the truth.

M: I do see it. That's the trouble. I'm so homely my father would pay a man to get me off his hands. Nobody wants me, Joe. I know that. I'm not blind.

J: I think you're blind. I think your father's blind, I think everybody in this town is blind. Maggie, you can be pretty, but you just have to try.

M: Oh Joe. Maybe tomorrow I'll wake up and I'll be pretty.

J: There are lots of other men, other than Jarrod.

M: Oh no there are not. Not for me. And I can't just spend my life waiting around for something to happen.

J: Maggie, will you stop feeling sorry for yourself? You don't have a man because you don't want one. Stop playing the wilting violet. Go out and find the man you want and let him know it. Go after him, Maggie.

Ben Cartwright sits in his armchair, bent forward, his head in his hands. Hop Sing bounces about him chanting a sing-song homeopathic mantra. Something is wrong with Ben, Our Father. When he woke, his head was larger than usual. It was about the size of a large world globe. Because of its new size, Ben's hairs were spaced further apart making it easy for Hop Sing to find evidence. He felt about Ben's head like a boy looking for a lost marble in the grass. Up near the hairline on his forehead Hop Sing found what appeared to be a large bug shell, brown and long like the egg sack on a cockroach. This caused a more intensive search for intruders. Ben himself found a large inflamed area. He pressed it from both sides which easily and smoothly began to force out the hind end of the cockroach creature. But it wasn't a cockroach, it was a long worm-like thing, about the size of a child's index finger and similarly jointed. When at last it was out, Ben and Hop Sing could see that it had a tiny human face that was busy contorting. Probably wasn't used to the bright lights. It was clearly not happy being out in the clear air.

Hop Sing says, "Oh my! This no hut you, Missah Caltwight?"

"No, Hop Sing. I hadn't noticed it," says Ben. Then he remembered the voices. The intrusive thoughts. They weren't thoughts after all. It was this worm singing in him, saying, "Excuse me, I must die now. Excuse me, I must die now. Excuse me, I must die now."

"Oh let's all feel sorry for Mistah Cahtlight. Fuck him and
his wormy head. He don't know pain. I'm the one with the
pain. Having to tell these dumb *Bonanza* stories. Just to get
even. This revenge is worse than the original grievance, for
Christ sake.

"The end of 'The Bridegroom'? Why you care? You so dumb
you can't figure it out? Okay, listen: Maggie and Little Joe
pretend to be courting in order to make Jarrod jealous which
he is and he punches Little Joe and runs off with Maggie.
Tuck is pleased that men would fight over his Maggie and
goes off to tell the boys at the Brutal Inn and Out.

"Now that's it, story's over. Get the fuck out of my face."

As the concluding credits roll, Wild Father thrusts himself
before them, like the bad kids at the Saturday matinee mug-
ging before the movie screen. He's playing air guitar. Actually, he has pulled his weirdly plastic penis out to an amus-
ing length with his left hand and pretends to do windmilling
Peter Townshend guitar strokes with his right. It's a good
imitation. The audience is all little boys and they're howling
with approval. He sings:

Wild Dad,
You make my heart sad,
You make life seem cheesy,
Wild Dad.

C'mon Wild Dad,
You make the world bad,
You're hooked by satellite
To everyone's favorite station.
Yea bad-ass Wild Dad.

COMBAT

1. In the episode of *Combat* titled "Command," my father was a German pontoon bridge built over a narrow French river. The bridge/my father threatened to provide a means of access for Krauts in order to roll their *Wehrmacht* machines into an area tentatively held by Americans. Therefore, as a strategic priority of the Allied forces, he had to be "taken out."

2. Until failures in North Africa and the Caucasus deprived Germany of the oil reserves needed for their "war machine," German tanks, planes, and armored carriers were feared and envied. They had the first "smart" weapons: guided bombs and the so-called V-2 rocket. They also had the first fighter jets (although by the time they became available there was so little fuel left that they were towed to the runway by cows). They were even able to synthesize their own gasoline from coal. In *Combat*, however, the function of these mighty war machines was merely to roar up, full of the empty ostentation of late-Wagnerian opera, and be promptly converted to something more like the discarded shells of cicadas. Brown and brittle things, buzzing in the wind.

3. My father felt a deep sense of shame, guilt, and humiliation for having provided the Germans this service. He gave his good, broad American back, fortified by Midwestern grains, to the purposes of the fascists. He knew it was a terrible thing to do.

4. The DSM III (*The Diagnostic and Statistical Manual of Mental Disorders*), under the heading "Diagnostic Criteria for Major Depressive Episode," states in B. 6. that the depressed patient has "feelings of worthlessness, self-reproach,

or excessive or inappropriate guilt (either may be delusional)." Was my father's fervently held notion, conveyed regularly during wee-hour confessions to his amazed and sleepy children, that he was a pontoon bridge for the Nazis delusional? Was Gregor Samsa's depressed ideation ("I am a monstrous vermin") delusional? Or were these things metaphors? Is a metaphor a delusion? Does the probability of Franz Kafka's depression require us to think less of him as an artist?

5. When I was a student at the University of San Francisco, I took an honors course in 20th century fiction. The course met at the professor's house. It was during the time when I first began to have opinions. My strongest and most perverse opinion, expressed in the lotus position from the floor of my professor's living room, was that Franz Kafka deserved no acclaim, was not to be admired, because the lone meaning his fiction had to offer was the effect of his own mental illness. What greatness is there, I demanded to know, in disease? What credit can one claim? My classmates and especially my professor were perplexed. How can you not like a story about a man who wakes up as a "monstrous vermin"? It is a magnificent metaphor! It is charming as heck! They were curiously unable, however, to find an aesthetic language to defend the beetled Austrian from my charge that he was just sick. I laughed as I debated, throwing their homilies back in their faces, and said, "Why should we claim to be pleased by this night, this paralysis, this human upon whom foreign objects grow?" But the real meaning of my laughter was, "Don't you see? This argument of mine is bug scales. I am Kafka. I am his disease."

6. My father was a lousy traitor and he knew it. Nonetheless, he felt an uncontrollable terror at the thought that the men he loved, *Combat*'s sturdy cast—Vic Morrow as Sergeant Saunders, Littlejohn, Caje, Kirby—were moving slowly in his direction, climbing through the brush, the dirty hills, and the curious eucalyptus trees misplaced in the French country-

side. These men were going to attach plastic explosives to his ribs. They had the little electric plunger for detonation. My father felt guilt, doom, and a hollow sense of justice. But he confessed readily that the squad, these grey heroic men, were right as usual. He should be demolished. Blown up before the Kraut treads could cross him. He was not only a bridge, but a bug. A monstrous vermin. A long bug like a walkingstick, a grim sort of mantis, extended across a French river. The German tanks would roll across my father's bug-back unless he was destroyed.

7. At the beginning of this episode, we learn that Lieutenant Hanley (Rick Jason) has been wounded and will be removed from ETO (European Theater of Operation) for thirty days. In his place comes one Lieutenant Douglas (guest star, Joseph Campanella). Unlike Hanley, this new lieutenant does not fraternize with the men. He gives orders. He doesn't smile. He eats his awful dog-soldier K-rations crouched by himself. Throwing down that abject meal, the Lieutenant orders one Pvt. Adams to burn a picture of his three-year-old daughter, a picture Adams has only just received from the States. Adams is offended. The squad is outraged. They do not like this new strong and silent lieutenant. His immobile face seems to take some dark delight in refusing them even the most basic human acknowledgement. They prefer their old lieutenant who seems by contrast a lieutenant of infinite smiles. One has to admit, however, that Adams had been warned to bring no personal effects. Well, hadn't he, soldier? No telling how "Jerry" would use this information if he were captured.

8. Adams was one of the replaceable squad members who rise glorious from the earth with each new episode only in order to provide fresh and expendable fodder for the Germans. How must these men feel? Do they recognize each other? Do they share looks with hurt eyes? Looks that say, "In this episode, amigo, we die, so that these others may find weekly prime-time glory." Do they resent Kirby or Littlejohn, off

whom German bullets, grenades and mortars bounce like popcorn? I confess to you that the deaths of those also-appearing-in-alphabetical-order affect me. My depressed brain, in which my ill spirit sobs in each blood cell, tells me that this is something worthy of tears. I weep for the lives of the soldiers who will not return in next week's episode.

9. Adams held the little photo of his daughter, tiny Brigette, between long thin fingers. His fingers did not wish to be burned. Kindly, he started the match in a far corner, distant from his baby's smiling head. But there is no mercy in fire. It leapt, accelerated by photo chemicals. In a moment it was over. Her charred remains lay on the ground. Her little smile lingered before him like an electronic afterimage. He had murdered his own child. He didn't deserve to live.

10. Of course, if he hadn't burnt his daughter, it might only have been worse. "I see, Herr Adams, that your little girl—Brigette, it says here on the back of this photograph in the hand of your lovely and tantalizing wife—has just turned three. Wonderful! Well, you know that little Brigette depends on you. She needs you to live. Yes! Above all else, live! She needs you to return home. She would not like you to die now for the silly reason that you will not tell us your soldierly objectives even when such information is of absolutely no use to us at all. Say, for example, that you told us that your mission was to kill the Führer. Goodness knows that we are aware that you would like to kill the Führer under the mistaken idea that we German people would stop trying to kill foreigners and inferior creatures without him. But that is wrong, as history will show, because in fact it is our innate sense of tidiness which compels us to clean up the awkward messiness of so many different colors and what have you. Different shapes. And sexes, *mein gott*. But we already know that you would like to throttle the Führer's long neck like a Thanksgiving goose if you could get your hands on him. But what of your wife and little Brigette? Your wife, for example, is clearly a very, what shall I say?, lovable thing since you

have plainly done something very unclean to produce this Brigette baggage. We Germans like to get behind and spread the woman's bottom and see all the dirty, hairy parts. This makes us sick of life and hence we must find all the unclean brown people in the world and kill them because they made us do it hindwise like a hound. Yes, there there, my friend, vomit. It makes you sick to think about. Well, it does me too. Here, I will vomit with you. Yaugh. Feels good, yes? To retch, ah, it is clean and bracing. Like your Old Spice cologne for men. Nevertheless, I promise you, I will find your wife after this war and spread her to find those soft and complicated things just as you Americans spread your fat Sears catalogues to find the colorful toys or the black and white women's underwear. Yes, there you have it. The big pieces. Of course, I will risk the impulse to suicide that such an act will inspire in me. I will transfer my desire to kill myself to your daughter. The only sad part, I think, with the children is the blood that comes from their tiny anuses. Is it not so in your own experience? Now, where do you come from and where were you going? Where is your headquarters? We wish to take a bite from that part of the map."

11. Were these possibilities part of the infinite despair that made Adams such an easy target a few moments later? He was killed by a German sniper. The hole in his forehead in fact looked like a bleeding anus. This is the despair that comes for these nameless men who are brought in fresh for each episode so that they might die from their nameless fears and from the tragic knowledge of their function in the *Combat* world.

12. Pvt. Adams, the original man. Brought onto the arboreal scene only to be promptly driven off again, in shame and despair. He must wonder, as he walks head down out of the studios, unemployed for the umpteenth time, "How am I different from these others? No one else is like me. I am uniquely flawed." There is no way of explaining it to him. He really is one of the world's chosen expendables.

13. "Command" is the first episode I've seen of *Combat* since I was a teenager, crouched like a little beast at my father's side, by the couch, where he reclined in much the same manner as the famous reclining Buddha. I thought at that time to be his henchman and recline on a couch in my turn. But I am halted in this destiny by the following question. Why am I breathing life back into this one episode, "Command"? What wild law of chance brought it to me? And yet it is the perfect episode for my purposes. Through it I intersect with the sublime.

14. And what of Sarge, whose last name never passes a man's lips? He too has *le masque*. He never smiled, never expressed any emotion except his determination to see his suffering through. And yet for a man who suffered, who had thousands of Nazi bullets enclose him (like the knife-thrower's assistant at the fair), he was strangely relaxed. He always looked sleepy. He leaned like James Dean against the window frame of an abandoned country cottage, his upper lip pooching over, and peered out into the world looking for the next Nazi needing a bullet. He was precisely "cool." Neither warm with life nor cold with death. Show him a horror, any horror. He will have no human response. Ghoulishness holds no terror for the ghoul.

15. A piece of trivia known only to the most ardent *Combat* fans: Sarge had letters tattooed on the knuckles of his right hand, DAS, and tattooed on his left, EIN. Kraut talk. Hey, Sarge, why you got Kraut talk on your hands? When he put his fists together, knuckles out, as he often did in the very eyes of the enemy, like Joe Louis in a pre-fight press conference with Herr Schmelling, the tattoos spelled DASEIN. Thus the subtle force of the terror he inspired.

16. During the skirmish in which Adams is killed, the Lieutenant is pinned down by German fire. He is behind a fallen tree or similar forest debris. (Why is it that in every episode the platoon is pinned down behind a fallen tree? And how is it

that the German fire from a machine-gun nest [machine-gun "nest": once again death in life is our theme] hits exactly an inch below the preserving limit of the tree? I think that the men of *Combat* could hide behind toothpicks.) As I say, the Lieutenant was pinned down. He escaped because—as always—his fellow Americans lobbed grenades with inscrutable accuracy into the machine-gun-birthing-place-for-birds.

17. In the end, the thesis of the television program *Combat* is that America won World War II because of baseball. It is finally the hand grenade that dissolves the impasse of mutual machine-gun fire that cannot hit anything. The GIs have good arms. The grenade is the size of a Grover Cleveland hardball. For Americans, the machine gun is merely "chin music." It keeps the enemy's head down. It is the fastball of the grenade that "punches them out," that "rings them up," that "sets down the side."

18. When the platoon reached the home of the French commando, Jean Bayard (who was to lead them to my-father-the-pontoon-bridge), the Jerries had already killed him. (My father felt a contradictory ecstasy: he might still live but his living would be one long treachery.) Sarge and Lieutenant took revenge on Bayard's German killers, but in the process made enough noise to summon the German platoons that were defending my father. They roared up in their *Wehrmacht* bug husks and a tremendous firefight ensued, rifles and varieties of machine guns making those deep, reassuring and compulsive sounds (the sound *ka-chang*, for instance) which my father worshipped.

19. My father would watch *Combat* obsessively if for no other reason than that he had an idolatrous relationship with the sound of guns. Knowing this, I've taken all my videotapes of *Combat* and transferred just the battle scenes to another tape which I will give to my father for his birthday. Recorded at the slowest speed, they will provide him with better than

six hours of bliss. My only fear is that he will die of this bliss, like the lonely masturbating man coming for six hours straight and discovering that it is his very bloody life that puddles on his stomach.

20. I am frizzled, stale and small.

21. There is an outstanding moral complexity to "Command." Lieutenant Douglas's sole desire (we discover late in the drama) is to return from this mission with all of his platoon members alive. For he was the famous commander of the legendary and ill-fated Mt. Chatel platoon which lost all thirty-one of its soldiers in the process of wiping out a whole "Kraut company." (This is the secret behind his apparent indifference to his men: he loves them too well.) It is for this reason that, when a German patrol strolls by, he orders that they be allowed to pass unchallenged. Allowing them to pass means, however, that his squad will not be able to take the road themselves. They'll have to go over hills and directly through brush. Tragically, it is this same German patrol that arrives at Bayard's and kills the valiant French patriot. Now the GIs must kill these Germans after all, as if for the second time, but for Bayard—the only man who knows the location of the bridge—it is too late. It is a world too late. He has been undone by the force of irony. Moments later, an "old man" is discovered wounded inside the cottage. He confirms new details of the above, to whit: Bayard was alarmed because Lieutenant Douglas was so late (late because he hadn't taken the road). Bayard wouldn't have encountered the Germans at all if he hadn't gone out to look for his old friend Douglas. Worse yet, Bayard is the last survivor, other than Douglas, of the infamous incident at Mt. Chatel. These are the fine, fine consequences of a single "command." They seem to expand and multiply like the hairline cracks in a porcelain glaze.

22. From this lesson we conclude the following disturbing truths:

    a) when authority is most brutal and indifferent, it is then that it loves and cares for us most;

    b) when one fails to choose death, death will come anyway, later, multiplied;

    c) ergo: always choose death.

23. Another way of understanding #22: in order to win the war, the Americans had to become the moral equivalent (as Field Marshal Reagan would say) of the Nazis.

24. "You know, Sergeant, I had to sit down and write thirty-one letters home to the wives and mothers of those men, I don't want to write any more letters. I can't."

    "Lieutenant, if we blow up this bridge, we might lose some men, but if we don't the Germans will use it. They might cut right through the whole division. If they do, how many officers will have to write how many letters?"

25. In viewing *Combat*, does one have to choose between the orgasmic, irrational bliss of gunfire and the complexity of the moral lesson? It would seem so. And it would seem that my father always preferred the merely darkly blissful, since I recall no post-episode explications of moral and dramatic ironies delivered to a silent son thirsting for enlightenment.

26. My father was a Romantic intent on sublime intimations; he was not a New Critic interested in formal device. These intimations came to my father, half-asleep in his dirty green recliner, as strangely as if creatures from outer space had come through his TV to deliver the news. A true oracle, the truth of the world visited him, virtually sat on his face, while he dreamed. This explains his patriarch's wrath when his children changed the channel in mid-program.

27. "What are you doing? I'm watching that program."

    "But, Dad, you were asleep."

    "Turn it back."

28. My father spent so much of his life in his green recliner

that it broke down subtly under his weight (my father was 6′ 4″, 220 pounds), never completely breaking but rather bending, collapsing earthward under his shape until, after twenty years of use, the chair itself resembled my father, as if it were an exoskeleton he'd left behind.

29. "It's been a long time since Mt. Chatel, my friend."

30. It turned out that the old man knew the location of the bridge. It was quite nearby. Sarge volunteered to creep to the bridge and blow it up while the rest of the squad occupied the stupid Keystone Cop Germans in their rattling bug husks who have surrounded Bayard's and abandoned their crucial duties at the pontoon bridge.

31. Understanding this neglect, my father feels an incredible anxiety. "Idiots and dumb cuffs. I'm surrounded by dumb cuffs." He is having a panic attack. With his feet on one bank and his fingers barely gripping the other, he is completely vulnerable. He wants to curl up in the fetal position, but that is not a posture pontoon bridges are allowed. In later years, during his son's time, there will be drugs for this disorder. Ativan, Valium. Drugs his son will take with gratitude. But for his own moment, there is only this enormous DREAD.

32. Sarge is up to his shoulders in the surprisingly warm river. (*Bien sûr*, this river heads toward the tepid Baja and certainly didn't begin in the Alps.) He pulls himself along the bridge from rib to rib pausing only to tuck the tender *plastique* between every other rib. It tickles my father a little, but mostly he feels the explosive's mighty and horrible potential. This feeling is much worse than the actual moment of becoming the meaty geyser that is his destiny. That, after all, takes only an instant. Spread across the sky, one has something of the nobility of a new constellation.

33. Done, Sarge crawls up on the bank and engages the little detonator. He depresses the plunger gently. The explosives

go off serially, one, two, three, four, like four strong spasms from a really good come. There is a different and dizzying camera angle for each new explosion.

34. My father would really have enjoyed these explosions/his death. But that contradictory pleasure would be like watching a snuff film in which you are the one to be snuffed. Would that turn you on, dead man?

35. As Sarge walks back to meet his platoon, he feels no joy. He'd done his job, saved lives by the bucketful, frustrated *les boches*, and yet he felt gloomy. He couldn't understand, of course, but he had become my father. My father's essence could not be destroyed; it had to reside somewhere. It must have flowed back up the wires to the detonator at the moment of his death. Like me, Sergeant Saunders is now possessed by my father. The undead. They walk among us.

36. When the Sarge arrived back, it was clear to all that he'd changed. He was not the same Sarge they'd known. But he couldn't explain anything, or he explained much more than his men, the gentle giant Littlejohn in particular, desired. Sarge said, "I know I am bad because I killed my father. However, I must be a little bit good because I feel guilty and am paying for it. If I didn't feel bad about myself, then I would be a completely wicked person. So leave me to my despair, I have earned it, and it is my only virtue."

37. "But Sarge, that wasn't your father," appeals our reasonable Everyman, the likable Kirby. "You just blew up a bridge is all." For Pete's sake. For cryin' out loud. For the love of Mike. You don't use your head, Sarge. Kirby looks around to the others, appealing to them for confirmation of this solid common sense. A tear trickles from the corner of the sentimental Littlejohn's eye. Caje puts a consoling hand on Sarge's disconsolate shoulder. "Vieil ami, nous voudrions t'aider," Caje says.

38. The riddle of the Sarge is undone when, to the astonishment of all (especially my father who pops up from his suburban recliner in awe), Sarge removes his helmet. Under his dirty, dented GI helmet with the chin straps hanging down most sloppily is not familiar blonde hair but a small patch of garden, mostly grasses and bright wildflowers. This grows out of the top of his head. The bright colors of the wildflowers make it appear that his brow is aflame.

39. "How did I do it? I took my bayonet and prepared the topsoil and then I sowed the seed. No, it didn't hurt too much. I didn't go very deep. Why? Don't you like it? Don't you think it's a nice idea to have a little garden on top of your head?"

GLEE

In the summer of 1963, I lived with my mother in a single room at the Nassau Trauma Center. The Center had as its intended function the emergency care of those who had suffered some heavy—and "traumatic"—physical wound. In Nassau, more often than not, this involved heavy bite marks, occasionally the entire removal of a muscle group—like the thigh, its tendons and tensors—from the bodies of those people who ignored the universally posted warnings not to penetrate beneath the water's surface.

In a better world, a place like the Trauma Center would not be necessary. There's no excuse for not understanding that fish live in these waters.

Neither my mother nor I had suffered any horrible injury. All our body parts were whole. Nonetheless, we were very promptly given a small room to share when we explained, to the nurse in Admittance, that "trauma" is German for dream.

She hadn't known.

In point of fact, if you can ignore the heavy reason for our presence in Nassau, we had it quite good. The room was warm, the hospital personnel courteous and often friendly, and I certainly had no complaints about the bounty of freshly prepared foodstuffs that were made available to us three times a day. It is true that the opportunities to enjoy these foods were frighteningly brief (on Tuesdays, for example, the breakfast period lasted from 6:15 to 6:25). But in a crunch, night or day, there were boxes of Rice Krispies or a can of Vienna sausages for the hungry.

But in general, our time was our own. Or nearly so. For it seemed that almost daily my mother was requested to contact the nasty, brutish little man in Accounts Payable. This was the only time during our long day that I was not immediately at my mother's side, ready to help her in whatever way I could. Even now, it is with some sadness that I remember her walking away from me, her sturdy, athletic legs propelling her down the long antiseptic corridor to that part of the Trauma Center which contained the administrative offices. Her legs often seemed to me to have a will of their own, as they separated two tender persons who would not otherwise tolerate separation.

Moreover, I didn't like the idea of her in the office alone with the little, grey man, tufts of hair sprouting unpredictably from his face. His skin like dirty parchment. And I am sure my father wouldn't have liked it at all. One knows how the mind of an accountant works. It's all dollars and cents with them.

As I say, these too frequent visits to the hospital accountant were nearly the only necessity in our otherwise long and free days. We were given the run of the trauma wards, could peek in whimsically on recuperating patients and friends, and always we were free to leave and stroll the long boardwalks down to the ocean beach.

In the afternoon, returning from our duties at the water's edge, my mother would remove her blouse and—asking me to shut tight my "peepers"—lie face-first on the bed. Then from the magical depths of her handbag I would retrieve a three-pronged "claw." It was years later, under the most intense diagnostic scrutiny, that I came to understand that this wicked object was, in fact, a sponge hook, used for prying sponges from their intractable places on the sea floor. (I accept, at last, a simple truth about the world: the sponges really wanted to stay where they were!) My mother called it simply her "back scratcher." In any event, I would pull the hook as gently as I could down her back. She moaned and purred, and this made me quite happy because it was surely the only moment of human kindness and warmth in our otherwise brutal days.

Only rarely would the hook catch in a wrinkle of flesh.

#

Sea Hunt 147

(Working title: "The Dark Evil")

Written by: Sloan Nibley

Voice-Over:

"I met Oliver Brandon and his daughter Lucille in the Bahamas in 1961. Brandon was the president of the famous Brandon Research Foundation, and he and his daughter were in Nassau vacationing. They were wealthy, very wealthy. But they'd worked hard for their money, and they'd earned this vacation. My job was to escort Oliver and Lucille in my boat, find the good fishing for them and discover sponge beds. I don't know why they wanted the sponges. What was it about sponges that made it worth hiring me and then risking their necks in the bottom of the sea? To this day, I ask myself this question.

"One morning I picked up Lucille Brandon at her hotel for a sponging date."

SHOT—LUCILLE AND MIKE, ON AFT-DECK IN TANKS AND SCUBA, EACH WITH A BAG ATTACHED TO WAIST-BELT (FOR SPONGES). LUCILLE IS "PRACTICING" INEXPERTLY WITH A WICKED-LOOKING THREE-PRONGED SPONGE HOOK.

" 'Is this how?' she asked me. She pawed the sponge hook as if she were weeding spring scallions. The acrid smell of onions was in the sea air.

" 'A little more like this,' I instructed, guiding her hand. She demonstrated the proper procedure, on her own. 'That's the idea. You're a quick study, you know that?'

"Lucille smiled, blushed and lowered her head. She was really very shy. Noticing this, I squeezed her hand, gently at first, as if to communicate my personal warmth, then more firmly, nearly to the point of pain. I watched her face carefully and just before her first wincing complaint, I released my grip and smiled.

"I'm Mike Nelson. Welcome to another adventure of *Sea Hunt*."

The real purpose of our visit to Nassau was simple if tragic. My mother was in love with my father, but my father was not with us. Not present to fill a warm space in my mother's bed, and not present to teach me about the rigors of a man's world. In his absence, we had little for which to wish, "no stars," as my mother quaintly put it, "to hitch our wagon to." She would really say that to me as we sat gazing out over the placid water, intent as if we stared down a dog by looking him directly in the eye.

It was my mother's belief that her husband, the man who gave her joy and me life, was under these waters. As you can imagine, this was a perplexing thing for a boy, even if I was by this time in my twentieth year, and thus on the cusp of all the knowledge and competence that manhood invariably brings. But at that moment, I may as well have been a squawking infant. The world had for me all of the interest of a very dry soda cracker. Even so, I managed to ask the obvious questions.

"Mom, why is Dad under the water?"

"Oh, Son, he's not happy. He's sad."

"Well, wouldn't he be happier up here with us?"

"It's hard to explain, dear. You'll understand in another year. When you're a man. But sometimes when people are very sad, they want to be alone."

"I guess there are lots of fish down there to keep him company."

"Yes, indeed," she replied, laughing at my childish associations.

Suddenly, a horrifying thought. "Mom, why don't the fish bite him like the people in the hospital?"

This question brought tears to my mother's eyes. She knew the horrible possibilities too well. For most people, going beneath the water's surface, to where the fish live, was something done briefly. A person became indifferent to her fate. She ignored the posted warnings. PELIGRO. ESTUPIDO. Bare legs went in up to the calves establishing the diagnostic theme of missing body parts. Then the sobbing plunge, the sudden, savage but tonic strike of the fish, followed by a lengthy, recuperative stay at the Trauma Center. One invariably returned with a positive if hardly "sunny" outlook, a clarified sense of one's place in the world (for instance, not underwater!), and a curving rim of scar tissue on the inside of the thigh—like a quiet, smooth worm sleeping just beneath the skin—over which the patient could run her fingers when she needed to be reminded that to be alive is an amazing thing.

But in cases like my father's, where a man has submerged himself for a period of weeks, then months . . . well, there was nothing therapeutic in it. Nothing bracing. And, let's be clear, the fish didn't give fucking about it. (Excuse me, but I am old enough now to use this bad word.) That's right. The fish didn't give fucking about it. If you were underwater, the fish would bite you. They would bite you and bite you. Therefore, the idea of life after months underwater was not a viable concept. No one understood what it could mean. To say, "My father has been underwater for months," had all the "meaning" of "My father has put himself through a meat grinder and turned the handle himself." Or, better yet, "Sealed bearing binder bolt father custom chewed." What my father had done could mean nothing either to the healthy or the ill. He was strictly unfathomable.

So I asked a different question. "How does Dad breathe underwater?"

To this Mom could smile. Now she was teaching me something. "It's very simple, Carl. He wears scuba gear."

"What's that?"

"A mask that goes over your face. A hose that goes into your mouth. A large metal cannister of air that is strapped to your back. Rubber flippers on your feet."

Now it was my turn to be horrified. I had never heard

anything so awful. Breathing underwater wasn't hard enough, so my father put a mask over his face? The idea of the human nose in this tiny space, shunted aside with the eyes in a glass-topped case, now in very ambiguous relation to the rest of the face, this was not something a person who wishes to live should do. The "air hose" running to the mouth was awful in its own way. Having made worthless the perfectly functional nose, human beings yoke large hoses, dwarfing the bronchial tree, a case of misproportion, of overwhelming the natural apparatus, and thrust them into the tiny human mouth. You can breathe with such a thing, I imagined, for an explosive gulp or two, but soon the tender, translucent bag of lungs rips. And why would anyone strap enormous metal cannisters to the back before entering water? You could hope to heft and balance them on shore, but once you've entered the water surely their gravitational charge takes over, flipping you and pulling you down like a tortoise who has run afoul of the Mafia. His shell is filled with concrete. See his little legs kicking as he hurtles toward the black depths of the sea? It's sad, I think.

Of the horror of one's feet replaced by rubber flippers, I believe I need to say very little.

My final question for my mother was this, "Is the reason Dad treats his sadness by putting himself far away from us, underwater, because we made him sad? Is it our fault?"

Obviously, my mother was impressed by the seriousness of this question. She looked at me sadly and, shaking her head slowly, said, "Not *we,* son, and not *our.*"

From which I drew the unavoidable conclusion, plummeting in my heart surely as my father plummeted in the sea: it was I who drove my father away.

He hated me.

"Once we were underwater, it became obvious to me why the Brandons, or anyone else, would want to look for sponges. It was beautiful down there. Colorful coral outcroppings made life charming. Extravagant fish cruising or darting furtively among the rocks made life intriguing. It was another world altogether. The sponge hunt was just a justification. Something to do.

"But this was to be no ordinary excursion for me or Lucille. When we reached the sponge bed, I noticed that she was behaving strangely. She acted almost defensively, as if she had something to fear from me. She held her sponge hook as if it were a weapon instead of a tool. Then, suddenly, it became a weapon and she came at me with it."

SHOT. LUCILLE AND MIKE STRUGGLE. OVERLAY SOUND OF RAPIDLY RELEASED AIR BUBBLES: OORKLE, OORKLE, SNOORKLE.

"I had all I could do to keep her from hurting both of us. Finally, though, I got her back up in the boat and out of her gear. At first I was angry because I felt this was a terrible betrayal of the sea world. But my attitude changed to sympathy when she said to me, 'Cold, cold. This is the end of the world! There's nothing left! Nothing!'

"She tried to jump back overboard and I grabbed her.

" 'Stop it now.'

" 'There's nothing left!' "

One day our routine was changed in a way I found very distressing. It was early in the morning, nearly 6:15 and I was hurrying to the cafeteria for my morning cereal. But my mother was spendng far too much time in the bathroom. She was carefully brushing her hair, applying lipstick and makeup. We would never get to the cafeteria in time.

"Mom," I said, "hurry up or we'll miss breakfast."

"You go on, dear, I have an appointment."

An appointment at that hour? All dolled up? I was suspicious, although, being a boy, I could hardly say of what. But I did run ahead, toast some raisin bread in the enormous eight-slice industrial toaster that always made me think of America as the land of plenty, and then returned to a corridor corner where I could watch her.

When she emerged from our room, she looked quickly and guiltily to each side and then walked rapidly toward the examination suites at the far end of the building. I had never seen my mother like this. She wore a tight skirt which hung to mid-calve but with a soaring slit in the rear which ran up between her legs, revealing to me giddy ripples of flesh. The stylish slit never really stopped but continued into a fold, the fold to a dart, the dart to a seam which concluded only once tucked inside an unimaginable crevice. Margarine, melting through my raisin toast, dripped down between my slick fingers.

She began walking toward the administrative offices and my first thought was, of course, that she had come to terms with the soiled accountant and his nasty double-entry ledger. But she veered off just before entering his corridor and went instead to an examination room.

The door was not open and not ajar, but there was an observation window and, sick with hurt, I went to it and peered long. No sooner was she inside than she began removing her necklace and bracelet and nice rayon blouse. The doctor kept his place before her, looking the very crippled image of scientific objectivity. But at just the moment that my mother would reveal herself to the man of medicine, her refreshing breasts available to him like a basin in which he might plunge his hands and face, she turned and presented him her back only.

His attention to her from that point was strictly medical. She showed him an awful, reddened and infected slice in the fleshy area just below her left shoulder. I could see him tsking his fattened tongue and applying his gentle fingers. Then he applied an unguent, a tropical salve. I didn't bother to wait for the inevitable questions. I knew them too well. This was my handiwork again. The perilous sponging hook in my immature hands had done this. Suddenly, my ears rang with my missing father's scolding words: "That's no toy, son."

I trusted my mother to protect me from the doctor's questions, although how she would explain such a thing I had no idea. What bothered me was that he'd probably say we should stop.

Not waiting for an end to this consultation, I went by myself to our usual perch at the water's edge. I sat at the very sandy brink and removed the shoe and sock from one foot. Although I knew this was no joking matter, I penetrated the oily surface with first one toe, then many.

I didn't know what sort of nibbling to expect.

Lloyd Bridges snuck back to his motel room as soon as the day's shooting was done. He might have gone out for drinks with members of the crew, all of whom, women and men alike, were young, beautiful and ornately tanned. They were giddy with the energy and money provided by the fledgling TV industry. He might have loaded himself with gin fizzes in the company of the key grip, the gaffer, or the best girl until they could all stumble to the producer's empty hotel suite in order to expose the shifting borders of shade and light on their browned bodies. But he had already pursued plenty of tan lines with a swollen tongue. He had other ideas now. Ideas which he shared with no one.

Before returning to his room, he walked furtively by the set and quickly filled a shopping basket with a few hurried shoves of his large hands. Once back in his room, he hung a sign on his door which read, "Temporarily absent. Stop knocking."

Trembling with anticipation, as if he were his own slim bride, he spread "Mike Nelson's" seal-grey wet suit out on the bed. The large glass diving mask was there as were the enormous rubber "flippers" and a snorkle which curled over his head like a question mark. Lloyd Bridges was beside himself with mad glee.

Quickly, he stripped out of his shorts, shirt and sandals. After a shower, he poured baby powder over himself, allowing it to drift down around his shoulders like snow. This was a happy man.

Then he began stretching the rubberized wet suit around his shoulders, the suit often slipping from his grip and slapping sharply at his skin. "Ouch," he giggled. He'd done the same thing a thousand times, as Mike Nelson, the famous TV adventurer on *Sea Hunt,* whenever an especially plump bottom presented to him the elastic in a clearly defined pair of panties. But this was different and better. For he was alone. He could do whatever he liked to himself and there was no one to object.

Finally, he was dressed. He had the flippers on and the mask and the snorkle rising above the curve of his skull, round as any sea lion's. He flip-flopped across the room, noisy like a little girl wearing thongs for the first time. Then, there before the full-length dressing mirror, he took it all in.

He was total. He raised his arms high in the air (or as high as the restricting rubber suit would allow him) and began dancing stiffly, hopping from foot-to-foot, laughing and hooting through the snorkle, the snorkle's little Ping-Pong ball spinning in its cage in pandemonious delirium. A strange sound escaped like a muzzy poot-poot.

This dancing, this flopping of flippers on the floor of his hotel room, this extravagant gladdening of his senses before the dressing mirror could have gone on. Gone on and on. For Lloyd Bridges had never before been this happy. Unfortunately, after a few minutes of his strutting, Bridges began to suffer from an excess of oxygen. He was hyperventilating. The room began to darken, as did the image in the looking glass. As the image dimmed, Bridges realized with the most extreme disappointment that it was not himself in the mirror. Not at all. It was the Creature from the Black Lagoon. A monster! But monsters were not allowed to make themselves happy. Monsters required victims for their happiness.

#

Soon I saw a dark form approach my proffered toes through the crystalline waters. It was a bottom-feeder, a saltwater catfish or carp, a species capable of eating—and digesting!—any noxious thing. It came forward, not like an eager and hungry predator, but dispassionately, almost bored, as if he were one of the poorly paid orderlies or technicians at the Center. He was just doing his awful job. I could just feel the sharp stubble of the creature's teeth when I realized something, no, everything. In a single moment, it all became quite clear. Panicked, I pulled my largest toe from the fish's dark and disappointed mouth.

This was all a goddamned joke. My father wasn't in these waters. In the name of God, how could my mother possibly believe that he remained under this awful water for months on end?

I don't know who told her this stupid thing, but she was a moron to believe it.

"I took Lucille to the Nassau Trauma Center where she was sedated and put to bed. Under the capable and caring scrutiny of the staff, six or seven of whom stood watchful at her bedside, Lucille improved. I can't say what it was they did to help her, but they chanted in a local patois, 'See things as we do, you are well. See things as we do, you are well.'

"I left Lucille to their care and went to the office of Dr. Clarke, who I hoped would have a diagnosis.

" 'Yes, Mike—those hallucinations of hers were chemically induced—no doubt about it. But from what source, I don't know.'

" 'Chemically induced—how?'

" 'Certain drugs—certain foods—contain chemicals called hallucinogens. They—'

" 'I remember—those magic mushrooms, down in Mexico.'

" 'Precisely. It's not very likely, though, that she ate any of those. Do you happen to know what she had for breakfast?'

" 'Well, they were going to have fish.'

" 'I thought so! Mike, last winter a new, very odd fish turned up in the Bahamas. The Indians have known about it for centuries. They call it "The Dark Evil." Here's a news story on it.

" ' " . . . when eaten by humans, it produces hallucinations of hopelessness . . . grief . . . despair. . . . The victim alternates between suicidal and homicidal impulses. . . ." That's it, Dr. Clarke! They must have caught just that kind of fish!'

" 'They?'

" 'Then her father's in the same shape she was! We've got to find him—at once!' "

CUT TO OLIVER BRANDON, LUCILLE'S FATHER, STORK-LIKE IN BATHING SUIT. HE STEPS OVER THE BODY OF AN UNCONSCIOUS GUARD, CARRYING A LARGE CANNISTER TO A BOAT. HE SINGS, "OH, THERE'S A FISH IN MY BRAIN, A FISH IN MY BRAIN."

ON THE SIDE OF THE CANNISTER IN BOLD LETTERS: **NITRO**.

When I returned to the Trauma Center, I did not find my mother in our room. Ordinarily, I would have been alarmed, but I was far too caught up in my sense of personal humiliation. We were fools. We stayed in an expensive hospital, where all the beds were needed for seriously wounded people, and why? So we could dream? That was an acceptable explanation to someone? So we could wait for my father, emerging from the lagoon of himself, to come up for air? Someone gave this silliness credence?

So I went from room to room looking, slamming doors, disturbing everyone's strenuous recuperation. At last I found her sitting on the bedside of Mr. Guava, who'd had a barracuda extract a chunk of flesh the size of a small rump-roast from his left side. Sagely, the teeth had stopped just before the kidney, although I'm told that the dark crimson color of that organ could be seen at the bottom of the bite. At any rate, he had become one of our favorites.

When my mother saw me, her face burst into one of her infectious smiles. She had been worried about me. "Carl! Where have you been?"

At first, I said nothing but sat simply in the stiff chair at their side. I was silent as judgment. Their warm human hands, which had been clasping, parted guiltily.

"Now, Mother," I began, "what is this business about waiting for my father to come up out of the water?"

She was perplexed. "Well, dear, I think you understand very well. This is something we do out of love and respect."

"Liar!" I screamed, jumping from my seat. I grabbed her wrist, spun her from Guava's bed and gave new marching orders. "Get to your room. I'll be there in a minute."

She went, tears and confusion already welling in her eyes.

I turned to our friend Guava to give him a word of advice, but he beat me to the punch. "Well, well," he said, "a little man at last."

I left then, crashing the door against its frame, but I found myself muttering, and knowing precisely what I meant, "Guava, you can suck my dick."

One afternoon the script girl, a young and very pretty girl, followed Lloyd Bridges back to his room. She had a lustful "thing" for Lloyd and was frustrated that he never stayed for the wet pursuit-of-tan-lines-with-engorged-tongues that invariably concluded the drinking of six ounces of Ron Rico. She longed to tell him that she was saving for him alone a special tan line. She wanted to show it to him so that he would see that it was in a dark and cool place where moist tropical ferns grew in profusion. But this opportunity never came because he always scurried back to his room, moving sideways like a crab, after a pitiful solitary rum and coconut milk.

But she knew that a man ought to like to lay his head
among cool ferns, so she followed him.

"May I come in?"

"Sure."

"I hope I'm not intruding or anything, but I never have a
chance to talk with you."

"Well, I'm usually pretty tired after a day of shooting."

"Oh, I know, but . . ." She notices the wet suit and
snorkle gear laid out on Lloyd's bed like honeymoon linge-
rie—"What's all that?"

"What?"

"This wet suit and stuff?"

"I don't know."

"You don't know?"

"No."

"Well, why is it here?"

"I guess I practice with it."

"You practice with it? What do you mean you practice
with it?"

"I don't know."

Then the girl saw the full-length dressing mirror and put
two and two together. It was five. She moved confidently
across the room and sat in a chair. She draped one tan leg
over the other and grinned. She felt masterful.

"Show me how you practice."

"Show you?"

"Yeah. Show me how you do it."

Lloyd blushed. She had him and she knew it. So she fig-
ured she could soften her demand a bit.

"Come on. Please. Really. I'd like to watch."

"You would?"

"You bet."

"And you won't touch?"

"No. Not if you don't want me to."

"And you won't tell anyone else?"

"Promise." She zipped her mouth closed. "Not a single
person."

So Lloyd ran into the bathroom and showered, dumped a container of baby powder over his shoulders and returned to the script girl. Quickly, he pulled the purplish sealskin around himself, the sea lion's cowl up over his head, then the mask and snorkle.

He looked dead into the dressing mirror and grinned. He raised his arms like two enormous vulture wings and began flapping them slowly, then the gradual rocking from flipper to flipper, the tempo slowly increasing to a stiff gallop. Happy. Happy.

The script girl was amazed. She put two fingers to her mouth, grabbed a bubble of spit, thrust the same fingers beneath her blouse and gave a wet pinch to a stiff nipple.

"Ummm.

"Ummm."

"I caught sight of Brandon just half a mile from his objective—the lighthouse, last glimmer of hope and sanity in our world. He was in a small launch with a puny outboard motor, so catching him in my powerful cruiser was no problem. Getting the nitro safely transferred to my hands was another matter.

"When Brandon realized he was being pursued, he panicked. He over-throttled the little Evinrude and stalled the motor. Helpless and drifting now, he yanked at the starter cord like a man in danger of losing his last pleasure.

"While he was distracted, I slipped into scuba gear and went over the side. My plan was to come up at his port, surprise him, and take control of the boat and its deadly cargo. The plan worked fine except for one thing: Brandon was not intending to wait for me. He put on his own scuba gear with the purpose of hand delivering the nitro to the feeble beacon. I arrived at Brandon's boat just as he was about to jump out. Emerging from the water, I saw Brandon standing at the prow, the nitro like a black hole in his side.

"Then, the worst: my image emerging from the dark water frightened him. He screamed out as if I were the monster from the Black Lagoon and not someone, a regular working guy, risking his life to save him. He lost his balance and tossed the nitro overboard.

"Instinctively, I pursued. The nitro's plunge was curiously lingering, gentle, not threatening. I should have caught it easily, but it seemed always to be just beyond my reach, while the explosive ocean floor beckoned immediately. I swam for all I was worth and as I swam words repeated themselves meaninglessly: the nitro is a black thought, the nitro is a black thought.

"I caught the nitro just before it struck the ocean floor. Overwhelmed, I sat with it on my lap, feeling its explosive destiny in my groin. I felt the implication of its center in my bowels.

"I was suddenly very confused about my act of 'heroism.' Had I saved something or somebody? Or had I simply failed to allow an intention to unfold itself truthfully?"

I packed my mother's belongings carelessly in the brown, ragged Samsonite case her father had given her as a high-school graduation gift. From the lobby, I phoned a taxi and gave the driver precise instructions about what bus my mother was to take to such-and-such a specified destination. Everyone acknowledged my authority in this matter. My mother stood silent and grave throughout the whole ordeal.

Curiously, as soon as she was gone I felt an irresistible need to return to the site of our innumerable ocean-side vigils. This, you will say, was thoroughly contradictory and, given my treatment of my mother, not a little hypocritical.

But emotions more primary than fear of hypocrisy were speaking to me. So I walked down the eroded path to the shore and sat on a sandy bluff about a hundred yards from the water.

While I was sitting there, the mythic occurred, natural

and inevitable as breath. My father emerged from the sea. He wore antiquated scuba gear, the stuff designed for WWII "frogmen." He seemed a little bewildered, unsure of what world it was that he had risen to the surface of. I am quite certain that he didn't see me, and surely didn't recognize me. Nonetheless, he removed his flippers and walked straight toward my perch.

In his arms he carried a large black cannister. A gift from the deep! A birthday present for me!

I stood and waved a single hand high over my head.

HAVE GUN—WILL TRAVEL

The return of sexual appetite is a sign that depression has begun to lift.

I. "HAVE GUN—WILL TRAVEL" READS THE CARD OF A MAN

A. *Proairesis*. It is 3 a.m. and Paladin is just returning—in top hat, cape and cane, string tie and spats—from an evening out in old San Francisco. He lives in a grand, elaborate Victorian hotel. Plush, velvety drapes cascade over every window. One imagines that they are dark burgundy or perhaps rich crimson in color.

As he makes his way into the lobby of this too-formal "home," he finds himself jostled, despite the late hour, by the lumpen-folk, the "rude." It is clear that the thought—"I could beat them with this ivory-handled cane"—crosses his mind. Or, in truth, he could shoot them. For he has a derringer, secret to the unsophisticated, but a lethal pint-sized death. He does neither. Instead, he sits in a grim loveseat and pours what is minimally the seventeenth cognac of the evening. (For most melancholiacs, alcohol is the self-medication of choice.) Suddenly, Hey Boy is at his side. "What's the matta you, Mistah Paladin?" he inquires with every appearance that he cares, in spite of the facts.

Paladin replies, "Have you noticed, Hey Boy, that there are too many people in this city?"

Hey Boy is puzzled. In China, it is the press of other people that provides a sense of the limits of one's own body. The idea of a person without a concept of the limit of his own body is deeply troubling to Hey Boy. In fact, the notion of a person who might like to be the entire world, in an extreme global solitude, is terrifying to Hey Boy. He hardly knows how to think this thought. This is why he doesn't spend a lot of time around Mr. Paladin. He gives him his mail, sends off the little dumb-ass cards, and leaves the gentleman in black with his high-class airs and violent habits to stew alone.

This evening, Paladin receives a letter from an old friend, Ernie Backwater, played by Harry Morgan. Ernie writes, "It's spring in Texas, the sky is clear, the trout are biting. Come and enjoy life. We'll go a-hunting."

B. *Figura*. He has just dropped off his daughter at the home of his ex-wife, the thought of whom makes him shudder with the acknowledgement that one has spent the last ten years in a perfect idiot's delight of self-mutilation. But now free of the cumbersome baggage of what is quaintly called "the past," he has only one thing on his mind. Her. He enters the crappy, hot student apartment he is obliged to live in for this summer *entre les vies*. She is watching a soap opera on TV, sitting in a kitchen chair, the junky TV on the kitchen table. (It's funny. Things that his wife did that he found contemptible, like watching TV, he finds charming and sweet in this new companion of his days and nights.) She wears only underpants and a T-shirt. He immediately walks straight toward her without comment or civility, exactly as he would if it were his intent to hit her. A puzzled if not alarmed look is on her face. Just as he reaches her, he drops to his knees, quickly pulls the underpants off her round thighs, and plunges his face between her legs.

A little later, she says, "All right. It's clear that we want each other almost constantly. From now on, when either of us comes through that door, it's open season."

C. *Exegesis*. A *paladin* is a knight or hero. It is especially that brand of crusader used by Christian morality and Western imperialism against the heathen (i.e. everybody-in-the-world-else). Richard Boone's television hero "Paladin" is, on the face of it, paradoxical. A gun-for-hire makes, as a rule, none of the moral judgments we expect of a hero. And this "good guy" dresses in black, as if anticipating Jim Morrison or punk rock. Furthermore, he wears a demonic icon, a horse's head (a chess knight), on his card, in the middle of his hat, and, critically, on his holster.

Hey Boy's fear of and hatred for Paladin had basis in a) Paladin's terrifying inability to imagine a limit to his own subjectivity, and b) Paladin's racist diminution of the Chinese in general and himself in particular to "Hey Boy." One evening as Paladin slept with his hat over his eyes, Hey Boy crept to his side. He pulled a carving knife from his ample sleeve. Before plunging it into the Western crusader, through some inexplicable and irresistible need, he raised the hat from Paladin's face. There he saw that high up on his forehead Paladin had his signature horse's head not drawn, not even tattooed, but literally branded deep into the skin so that its outline seemed to rest on the cranial bone itself. It glistened like a mystic third eye. Hey Boy (in a reaction Paladin will understand per force as that of a benighted, childlike and superstitious Oriental) imagines that Paladin can in fact see him with this "eye." He shrieks, drops the knife, and runs off babbling in his implausible Cantonese. Paladin opens his real eyes, raises from the divan and laughs deeply, the laugh pursuing Hey Boy like pure terror. He removes from his forehead the astonishing device which he acquired during his deep study of Ficino's *Hermes Trismegistus*, the obscure bible of the occult neo-Platonic movement in fifteenth-century Italy. Surely, he is awesome for knowing that Hey Boy's premeditated act was coming his way. More awesome for his access to this knowledge. But one would be wrong to think that he was brave to execute this stratagem. Bravery and contempt are different.

In Paladin's relation to Hey Boy, the puzzle of the master-slave relationship is resolved. The enduring enigma of the master (the so-called "misery of mastery") is that his domination of the slave provides for the master the pleasure of consuming the fruit of someone else's work. The pleasure of "making" is denied the master. He is left out. Even his consumption is of something empty since he cannot understand what it is that he consumes.

But Paladin has cut through this knot most brilliantly.

Not only does he have the fruit of Hey Boy's mostly worthless work (he carries telegrams on a little silver plate) but he also retains for himself the privilege of all action. It is Paladin who rides off on adventures, who holds the secret of all *savoir faire* like a bloody pomegranate seed, violent and recondite, caught between his teeth.

For Hey Boy, as for me, our lives are all incapacity. "No, no, no. That's not how you do it, boy. Give it to me." Fixing the car is "knowing" how to hold the screwdriver or whatever other tool the master (obdurate father/hero) might someday need. But even at that the idiot son fears he will fail and the screwdriver will tumble from his sodden fingers.

If one is very blessed, one at last learns a skill, the one skill without which no other skills can follow: patricide. Yes, one day Hey Boy and I will take our revenge.

II. **A KNIGHT WITHOUT ARMOR IN A SAVAGE LAND**

A. *Proairesis*. When Paladin arrives in the little Texas town in which his old friend Ernie Backwater lives, he discovers that Ernie has lured him there falsely. He has no intention of fishing (he only said that they were "biting"). And the only hunting he considers is, not for deer, but for a man. This hunted man lost his son to five murderers (although his son was murdered only once). This man killed the five, but, *malheuresement!*, the *wrong* five. As if to demonstrate that his commitment to this false path was no superficial thing, he then murdered a member of Sheriff Backwater's posse, a deputy, and he even shot Ernie himself in the stomach and "left him for dead." Ernie says, "The Comanches have a name for the kind of Texas man who drove the Mexicans out of this state, drove the Comanches into the Apaches, the Apaches into the Cuyashawas and the Cuyashawas into the plains. *Americano fiero.* American Savage." Paladin, as if to show he hasn't ridden his horse over a thousand miles from San Francisco just to have a hayseed like Ernie give things their truest name, declares (without ever having met this man; knowing nothing more than this thirty-second anecdote provided by Ernie), "That's not a very good translation, Ernie. It's not *American savage*. It's more like *American primitive*."

Hey Boy and I sit wrapped in each other's arms before the television screen, bewildered. What can Paladin mean? What is this fine distinction? Grandma Moses was an American primitive, but this guy has to be something else. By *primitive* he is, no doubt, alluding to some of the same human features that made his fellow guests, in the San Francisco hotel, "rude." The rude or primitive or uncivil here stands for all those not learned in the highest European culture. But this guy has killed seven people. That's just primitive? Rude San Franciscans and murderous Texans are alike in that they are in the way of the creation of a world in which no one touches anyone else, a world in which people glide by each other sleek and spectacular as rare fish.

This scene is deeply perplexing for other reasons. 1) In fact, the Spanish for "savage" is *fiero*. "Primitive" is *primitivo*. What is Paladin trying to obscure with his fraudulent pedagogy? Why does he fear the concept of the American savage? Who is the American savage? Paladin himself perhaps? 2) As often as I rewind and replay this scene, I cannot find in it the word *Americano*. Is this simply because they have unspeakably bad pronunciation? Or is it because they are really saying what in fact it sounds like they are saying: *amante fiero*? Savage lover.

The savage lover is a man like Paladin who touches no one, not his wife, children or friends. His only human contact is explicit in the tidy derringer that creates a parenthesis at whose far reach is a bullet. It is how one loves a world that one finds disgusting, repellant.

B. *Figura*. It was not long before this "open season" on the discreet inside of their student-apartment dungeon became a truly "open" season outside as well. When they drove together in their car, one or the other or both had genitalia available for grateful caress. When they went to movies, she wore a light dress and no underwear. For that season of their intimacy, even Hollywood seemed interesting. Movies of the period, like *E.T.*, had not only their own dumb charm, but the inexhaustible rhythm of orgasm. Hollywood plots became magical. In *The Natural*, when Robert Redford hit a home run, he ejaculated. In *Tender Mercies*, when Robert Duvall spoke quietly of his hard life, it was a miracle and a mystery because he was having multiple orgasms. Or so it seemed to their hormone-saturated memory.

Very soon, wherever they went, they were able to smell themselves. The car upholstery, the seats at the movie theater, the blotter on his office desk, the carpet in certain dark corridors of the library. And anything they happened to touch was "enriched," so thorough had the aroma of their mutual regard become, as richly subcutaneous as if their fingers had been soaked in rum, like extravagant bonbons.

He dared to think, through this joy, "We have claimed the world as our own."

C. *Exegesis*. It is time to speak of Paladin's erudition. At first it seems a good thing because for once it appears that there is a television drama which honors knowledge and intelligence. It is the fact that Paladin can claim to have read Leonardo's scientific notebooks and can find that difficult knowledge useful in weekly episodes and applicable in a world of cowpokes that gives him his crucial "difference."

This quality, "intellectual superiority," was not lost on his commercial sponsors. PALL MALL cigarettes argued, "Wherever you find particular people, that's where you'll find PALL MALL cigarettes." (This "particular" commercial was set at a steeplechase, where apparently many of *Have Gun*'s fans congregated on weekends. In the background, a fey woman in jodhpurs successfully launches an enormous stallion over a fence.)

PALL MALL produced "famous cigarettes." (Of what did its fame consist other than its famousness?) "Its natural mildness is so good to your taste." (Good to your taste? Did your father ever say to you, "Here, Butch, this beef jerky is good to your taste"?) "The reason why? Smoke traveled through fine tobacco tastes best. PALL MALL's famous length travels the smoke naturally." (Is four inches a "famous length"? Do you "travel your feet" when you walk?)

PALL MALL is the country cousin who merely apes in an obvious way what seems to come naturally to "the Real Thing" (always an imitation of an imitation). Because of its jejune presentation, it reveals not only its own internal flaws but the flaw in the seamless logic of Paladin as well.

For he too is all tautology! He is erudite Paladin because he is erudite Paladin! I yam what I yam! No better than fucking Popeye!

But what of my own intellectual performance here? I am writing about a TV cowboy show but I use words like *proairesis, figura,* and *exegesis*? As my mom would say, I am "Mr. Smartypants." A snob.

Is this not a way of demeaning popular culture and the entertainment it provides? Do I not seek to demonstrate my own "difference" and thus the distance at which I stand from ordinary people and their world? More to the point, do I not distance myself from my father, who watched these programs?

When I was nineteen years old in the summer of 1970, at the end of my first year in college, I also worked for the local draft-counseling office, organized and run by the five or six Marxists living in San Lorenzo, California. My father and I argued endlessly about my pacifism and anti-war activities (my mother wailing in the background, "Oh where did we go wrong?"). I remember on one night in particular we argued about whether I would be "allowed" to go to the Oakland Induction Center to leaflet the recruits as they got off their buses and made ready to take that ominous first "step forward," the second of which might land them in a rice paddy in Vietnam. The TV was on, my father was in his recliner, aimed toward the TV but with his head directed back toward me. I wasn't going. No son of his da-da-da, predictable-WWII-pro-patria-father-spiel.

Without forewarning, I launched into an elaborate, syntactically bone-jarring, personal, historical, political, cultural and religious critique of the war in Vietnam, replete with many of the splendid Latinate words I had been made familiar with at my Jesuit lair (where I studied the most *re-cherche* weaponry for patricide, viz., words like *plethora, na-dir, ambivalent,* and *ubiquitous;* as in the telling phrase, "the reason North Vietnam succeeds in the war is that Vietcong supporters are *ubiquitous* in the south." That's *ooo-bee-qwee-toos.*)

My father was neither enlightened nor amused by my callow performance. His response was, "You talk like a damned computer." Which was a way of saying—"You are not human."

In fact, this "fiction" is an orgy of dehumanizing gestures. I am not human to my father, the gooks are not human to the United States military, no one is human to Paladin, and, stealing a page from Paladin's book, I find my father inadequately vocabularied for my own evolving sense of the human. In short, in this world life is all death because no one recognizes anyone else as human like themselves. Everyone seems to aspire to death. And it's a veritable Gettysburg of likely candidates.

III. **HIS SIX-GUN FOR HIRE GREETS THE CALLING WIND**

A. *Proairesis.* Three months later, we are told, Backwater and Paladin finally come upon the American primitive. He sleeps beside his little cowboy campfire. Paladin argues, wrongly, that it is just a "rag doll." (The Nazis called their Jewish cargo "puppets.") The savage himself, Paladin continues, is in the bushes, indifferent to sleep. Paladin and Ernie creep up on him anyway, rag doll or no, but step on way too many crunchy twigs. Mr. Primitive awakes and blasts Paladin in the left shoulder. Paladin returns the favor with two bullets in his shoulder. The Primitive is now captive.

We have been led to expect that this Americano is "like a force of nature . . . pestilence, drought, famine." Imagine our keen disappointment and contempt when it turns out that this "force of nature" is only Robert Wilke, a large, loutish, talentless B-actor that we have seen on every variety of TV serial. We think we have seen him on *The Untouchables,* boring, virtuous *Wagon Train,* and maybe even as a wholly insincere "bad guy" on *I Love Lucy.* He doesn't really scare even Lucy Ricardo, let alone Paladin. He is not a force of nature: he is a force of televisual cretinism.

Unhappily, this confirms the suspicion of incompetence we entertained when we saw that even Paladin's old friend Ernie was just Detective Frank Smith from *Dragnet.* Or Major Potter from *M*A*S*H.* What in the world was he doing in Texas in the 1890s?! Were we really supposed to pretend we didn't recognize him? "Oh, look, now I'm a cowboy!"

B. *Figura.* Once she took him home to meet her parents. He was surprised to see that, although she was of a slightly younger generation, her family too was all life-on-TV. Even her father slept away his life, dreamless, in a recliner before the TV set.

One night they were curled together on the couch, covered by her mother's afghan. (Her mother had actually thrown it over them, before going off to bed, commenting that they might be cold.) The father snoozed, while late-night TV produced reruns of *Mannix* and *Hawaiian Eye* one after the other. Then, with the inspiration that was only typical of them at the time, his hand found its way under her pajama bottoms. Soon, she quite insisted that his cock find its way to where his fingers had been. Now life-on-TV proceeded but everyone, old guard and revolutionary alike, had his eyes closed. (What does it mean that TV achieves its ultimate purpose when it is watched with eyes closed?) In spite of the intense pleasure this moment offered him, he couldn't help thinking of their fucking as something dangerous, as an attempt upon her father's life perhaps. Wasn't one of the ancient Greek laws of hospitality "You will not fuck your host's daughter under his nose"? Those who ignored such laws usually ended up rueing the day.

Just as he prepared for the last few silent, risky thrusts that would send him into bliss, he opened his eyes. There before him, just the other side of the particleboard coffee table, stood a man in black, a prissy Van Dyke mustache decorating his upper lip, and a revolver in his outstretched hand, pointed dead at him. He cocked the hammer. The man in black fired the gun twice and two bullets ripped through his left shoulder. He is astonished that this has happened and astonished that he is not dead. Why this destructive generosity?

"That last shot . . . you could have killed me."

"That's right."

"I put one in your shoulder and you put two in mine."

"That's right."

"I wouldn't have done that. I would have killed you."

"I know."

"Will it hurt when they fix it?"

"Like nothing ever hurt before."

Thus distracted by both wound and conversation, he has gone limp just when he should have been most firm.

She turns her head back towards him and whispers, "What's the matter, honey?"

C. *Exegesis*. The essence of the father is fixed nowhere. The father is the son. The father is a "six-gun for hire." The father is a prissy mustache or a pack of famous cigarettes. The father is an "economy," a set of human relations that works (even if its working is all a process of damaging; damaging the already damaged, a second bullet hole in the shoulder). Even Paladin must live this truth. One night, during their long trip home with the so-called Primitive, Paladin and Ernie talk. They are under blankets, side-by-side. This is cowboy pillow talk. Paladin asks Ernie questions about this man they are returning for hanging. They are plainly the innocent questions of a boy. Paladin is Ernie's son.

"Ernie."

"Yes."

"You say his son was murdered by five men."

"That's right. For a ten-dollar gold piece his Pa gave him for his fifteenth birthday."

"And he hangs for that?"

"For revengin' his son? No. He killed the wrong men, Paladin."

"Does he know?"

"No. Now go to sleep, we've got a long day ahead of us to-morrow."

"But I'm not sleepy."

"Paladin, close your eyes and go to sleep."

IV. **A SOLDIER OF FORTUNE IS A MAN CALLED PALADIN**

A. *Proairesis*. Ernie, Paladin and the Primitive have at long last returned to the little Texas town where the Primitive must die. A noose greets them suspended above Main Street as if it were this town's corporate logo.

The Primitive is now a different man. He accepts the requirement of his death. He asks Paladin for one of his beautiful cheroots and smokes it with the gusto, *un peu triste, bien sûr,* of a man at peace with himself and his world. They go to the barbershop for a "barbershop bath" and shave. "There's nothing like a barbershop bath," says the Primitive. "I almost feel like a new man." Can this be that same bad person who killed seven? *Mais cette homme ici, il n'est pas un sauvage!* Thus the effects of even a brief exposure to Paladin's civilizing force.

While he is being shaved, the Primitive asks to see a newspaper. "Something to read." The marks of his emerging civility are overwhelming. A great curiosity about his world has emerged in him, even at the very moment that he is about to be made irrelevant to that world. Tragically, the story in the paper that the barber hands him is about the escape from a Mexican prison of the five true killers of his son. He now knows a) that he killed the wrong men, and b) that the murderers of his son are again at large.

This is a powerful crossroad for the Primitive. Which will be the stronger force? The moral certainty of the futility of his revenge and grief over the innocents he has slain? Or the resurgence of intoxicating revenge?

As it is said on life-on-TV, "We don't have to wait long to find out."

While he is being shaved, the Primitive takes the razor away from the barber and puts it to the barber's throat. A reason to live has surged through the Primitive. He has miles to travel and badder men than himself to kill. The Primitive takes their guns and leaves, reasonably requesting that they not do anything foolish.

(A problem in dialectics: if he were still thoroughly the Primitive, "a force of nature," he would simply have shot Paladin, Ernie, the barber, and the first six or seven people he saw in the street. He could then have easily escaped. However, in a gesture that can only be described as humane, he allows his "friends" to live, apparently because he doesn't wish to kill more innocents. He not only leaves Paladin alive, but he expresses a [limited] concern about his future through his lame appeal to "reason" [don't do anything foolish]. The curiosity here is that because of this germ of civility, he himself will die. So, he dies not for being thoroughly the Primitive, but for being only partially civil. Ironically, he would find that if he were thoroughly civil, like Paladin, he would then be able to kill and take revenge with impunity, just as Paladin is about to do with him. Thus, the purest desire of the Primitive [to kill without consequence] is realized in the highest achievement of the civil.)

It is in the nature and tragic fate of Primitives never to know enough, never to be thoroughly aware of the resources of the civil. For Paladin has his derringer tucked away beneath his belt. Not so hard to find, really, but for the Primitive as probable as keeping a poisonous toad in your trouser pocket. ("All right, Paladin, throw down your gun. Slowly. Now, do you have any poisonous tropical toads? Put those on the floor too.") Of course, any twelve-year-old boy watching the show could have told him, "Hey, you forgot Paladin's derringer! Everybody knows that Paladin has a derringer! How can you be so dumb?" It is finally only a matter of time until the Primitive is asked, "Display your stupidity. Now . . . die for it."

B. *Figura*. One hot summer afternoon, they were at a backyard barbeque. The others, their friends, none of whom had they seen in months, had minds for volleyball, food, music, and conversation. Our heroes, on the other hand, merely chafed under the limits of acceptable behavior such outdoor gatherings with curious friends allowed. They held hands or touched a knee, but this was hardly adequate to their great and reciprocal need. They wanted to *touch*. The full-body touch. So, whispering like conspirators, they decided to leave this party, although they'd only just arrived; hadn't even eaten a corn chip. They would return to their apartment for a solid blunting of their always sharp appetites, then they might come back for some croquet or a half-hearted assay into the culinary delights of the cheeseball. As they pulled away, their friends stood in the front yard, staring, a couple mouths agape, one or two of the more astute whispering in excitement, all of them thinking, "My God, in moments they'll be doing it again. They can't keep this up! They'll hurt themselves!"

Once home, they went immediately to their bedroom. She took off her shorts and blouse, but he was frozen by something. The man in black. He had returned. He'd been trailing them for months. He was dogged, determined, and thoroughly professional. And now he reclined on their bed, his hands behind his head, his hat with the silver horse's head—decapitated, mutilated—pulled down over his eyes.

She noticed that something was wrong. "What's the matter, honey?"

"It's the man in black. The one who shot me in the shoulder at your parents' house. He's lying on our bed."

"Oh, come on," she sighed, grabbing his hand and tugging him toward the bed. "Don't be a jerk."

"No!" he shouted. He pulled his hand violently from hers, ignoring the fact that "jerk" is one of those words that lovers call each other when things are really not going so well.

She was freaked. She considered the "you-fucking-stupid-asshole" response. She was not, by her own description, a particularly nice person. She was in this relationship because it was unbelievably exciting, and she was in love. But this story—about losing his erection because "her father" (disguised as a cowboy gunslinger) had shot him in the shoulder—was really annoying. One tolerates the occasional moody stumbles of one's lover, right?, but this was stupid.

A little pulse of angry flame surged up in her, but she quickly capped it with sweet and comic indulgence, although it wouldn't be very long at all before this ambiguous "little flame" would lead her to bed with others-not-our-hero and the end of this summer idyl. But for now, she worked in his interest. Naked, she reached into her crotch and pretended to pull out a gun. She jumped back and pointed it at the mysterious bed.

"Okay, mister, the fun's over. Not as smart as you think, are you? Didn't know I had this." She smacked her pubis with the flat of her free hand like she was smacking a horse's hindquarters. He was astonished by this turn of events. Truly, she was the most amazing lover he had ever known. "Don't do anything foolish," she said. "Think you can take me? It doesn't have to be this way."

As if responding to her remarks, a little annoyed that his nap had been disturbed, the figure in black raised his hand to lift the hat from his eyes. For that moment it was no game of pretend she played. No cowboys and Indians romp in the yard. No theatrical indulgence of a neurotic lover. She actually seemed to see the killer too. She was alarmed by the implications of accepting his gaze. And for good reason. We might recall what happened to Kama, Hindu god of love, when he disturbed Siva's meditation on Mount Himalya. He was burnt to ashes by Siva's third eye! If the traveling gun-for-hire set his eyes on hers, locked them in, she was a goner. "You idiot," those eyes would say, "put that thing down. You don't know how to use it. That's not a toy."

"Blam! Blam!" Her breasts jumped up in surprised recoil from the force of the shots. She screamed, frightened by the intensity of her own play.

Having done what had to be done, she could now turn to her amazed lover and smile. She held out her hand that was a gun but was now again her hand. She pulled him gently toward the bed. The body was still there. She surely had killed him dead though. Fearless, she lay back into the black figure as if it were a cocoon. She brought her lover up on her, then reached into his shorts. She smiled and said, "I love you."

He smiled and cupped her face in his hands. "Thank you. You saved my life. How can I ever repay you?" She laughed, all joy returned. "Just doin' my job, mister."

They seemed to sink into the black body, and as they did the dark hombre dissolved in a powdery mist around them. The mist became large black ostrich feathers like the dance-hall ladies wore in Victorian San Francisco. The feathers enfolded and caressed them.

C. *Exegesis*. Pop. Pop. "Whiskey, Ernie."

The death of the Primitive at the hands of the Civil, touched by the tiny fatality of the derringer, is a deeply encrypted trope. Taken literally, it implies the mean continuation of a culture of violence, alcoholism and inhuman isolation. Taken figurally it means SEE WITHOUT TURNING AWAY. DO NOT FORGIVE THE UNFORGIVABLE. STAY ANGRY. IT IS OUR ONLY HOPE.

It was, for the boy, the gray repeatable night . . . shocking . . . that little pre-fab mousehole they lived in . . . and his Mommy and Poppy, such dirty stinkers . . . measly is the word for it . . . the family thoughts filled the house like farts . . . thicker than Poppy's cigarette smoke . . . never opened a window summer or fall . . . neighbors were glad for that, let me tell you . . . measly's the word all right: small, dingy, deformed . . . imagine the foulness . . . they had venetian blinds . . . the boy wrote filthy slang in the dust—"pee-hole" . . . a year later you could still read it, the letters filled in with more recent filth, like a footprint filled with new snow . . . ferocious! . . . thirty years and never dusted once! . . . they had a dog, a little cocker spaniel . . . but its fur was so matted that giant clumps stuck out at bizarre angles as if they were deformations . . . new doggy appendages . . . weird! . . . couldn't tell which way the dog was going . . . it seemed constantly to be snarling out of its asshole . . . they needed a private sewage treatment plant for all of the shit that little sweetie piled on the tiny patio . . . unbelievable . . . this dog was the anti-Christ! . . . turned loaves into shit . . . imagine a mountain of the stuff out there . . . maybe that's why they kept the windows closed . . . no one went out except Poochie . . . he'd move to-and-fro before his masterpiece . . . you could only tell if he was walking forward or backward if his tongue happened to be hanging out . . . otherwise he was just this irritable dust rag that watched over a pile of crap as if it were the Taj Mahal . . .

Forget the dog! . . . there's more . . . evening . . . that was the time when the family was truly itself . . . during the day the kids went to school, Mommy went to her job at the Doggy Diner, and Poppy went off to do whatever he did . . . I'll tell you what he did, he played pool, drank Old Crow, and slept in his car . . . but beginning with dinner, they were a real family . . .

No one knew how to cook . . . they'd eat the most unbelievable junk . . . spectacular . . . worse than the dog . . . they kept their food piled in boxes in the pantry . . . freeze-dried turkey tetrazini . . . freeze-dried chicken almondine . . . loathsome . . . someone would boil a pot of water . . . each portion got a half-cup of water and began to grow . . . it was like eating sea monkeys . . . unbelievable, really . . . less than human . . . you should have seen them at the table . . . heartbreaking . . . there was a pile of Wonder Bread and the cheapest margarine you can imagine . . . came in gallon tubs . . . the manufacturer didn't even have the decency to dye it yellow . . . it wasn't something to eat, it was an expression of contempt . . .

The children were growing up idiots . . . the boy stayed in his room generating his private adolescent stink . . . his younger sister found little boys, charming innocent kids, really, nice as you please, and took them into the bathroom with her . . . and she did everything . . . hung her ass out the bathroom window, spreading her cheeks and screaming with maddened delight . . . the boys could put anything in there . . . she was a wonder . . . Ping-Pong balls, Ken dolls headfirst all the way to his little sneakers, Parcheesi pieces . . . the boys played a game called can-you-guess-what-falls-out . . . the most abominable childhood . . . little boys in the neighborhood talked about her for generations, a legendary nasty girl . . .

Her brother was the jerk-off crown prince . . . his pajamas were stiff like cardboard from all the spunk he spilled on himself . . . you could patch a wall with them, you could patch a furnace, you could use them to repair heat-reflecting tiles on rocket ships . . . and the piles of stuff on his sheets were like amber deposits . . . domestic bug life got caught in it . . . house flies lost their lives in the sticky mess . . . nothing pretty about it . . . he walked through his little existence smelling of rotting mushrooms . . .

After dinner, the real action would begin . . . the TV . . .

Poppy would watch "his show" . . . "my show is on," he'd say
. . . as if that made it special . . . the old meany . . . every hour
of every evening was "special" because "his show" was on . . .
this is not something people accept anymore . . . times have
changed! . . . we're more democratic . . . we don't put up with
these tawdry patriarchs . . . but in his moment he had exclusive claim to watching *Combat, Bonanza, Highway Patrol,
Sea Hunt, Have Gun—Will Travel,* and many more any time
he pleased . . . anything with guns in it . . . the amazing thing
is, he slept through every damn one of them . . . could hardly
make it through the credits . . . by the end of the first commercial he was out . . . but the bombs must have comforted
him, like synthetic orgasms going off in his pineal gland . . .
what an unbelievable stinking mess of a human being . . .

And the fudge! . . . every night Mommy made fudge . . .
whole plates of the stuff . . . sweet enough to lock the brain
. . . the sugar would open Poppy's eyes for a moment . . . you'd
see some suffocated angelic creature deep in his blue iris
screaming bloody murder . . . and then, wham, gone
. . . dead to the world . . . the kids of course would zing off the
walls for fifteen minutes, then retreat to their respective
rooms . . . sudden sugar autism . . . they needed whatever
tingle of pleasure might make them feel even a little less
than dead . . . little sis would be whamming Mr. Potato Head
into her cunt . . . he'd be jamming and whacking his little
whistle against the pile of amber under his sheets . . . no
pleasure in any of this, mind you . . . this was pure childhood
desperation . . . and poor Janey, saddest of all, left standing
silent in the living room, a most bewildered orator . . .

Each night a new plate of fudge . . . of course, the old plates
would pile up, the leftover candy turning to crusty rock . . .
Poochie would lick it until his tongue bled . . .

This was life for nearly two decades . . . it could have gone
on forever, not like the worst but the most embarrassing
circle in hell, had not the children come rattling out of the
house at eighteen like loaded dice . . .

"Time to go to college," Poppy said . . . heaven knows where
he got that one . . . that was a good one . . . what university

would take those in-turned abominations? . . . Jesuits took
the boy . . . hovered around him, at first dumbstruck by the
absence of human attribute . . . it was a trippy sight for a suburban boy, too, the priests in their gowns . . . they made him
take his hand off his dick straight away—proximity to sin
indeed! . . . spoon-fed him Aquinas . . . next thing you know,
lo!, he's stopped that irritating quacking that drove his public school teachers mad . . . he'd have flunked every level he
was in if his teachers could have faced another year of his
non-stop quacking . . . quacking, goading erections out of the
top of his denims, and trying to put his lunch inside girls . . .
I'm not kidding . . . tried to put a baloney sandwich inside
Julia Pacheco . . . she asked, "Me quiere mucho?" . . . poor kid
. . . fucked-up as he was . . . anyway with the Jesuits he
started making human sounds . . . "summum" . . . "bonum"
. . . believe me, people were quite impressed . . .

There was only one night in two decades that was other
than sepulchral . . . tenebrous . . . when things are tenebrous,
you don't even want to know how dark they are . . . even the
darkest human life has at least one moment of revelation in
it . . . "What's on TV tonight?" the boy asked . . . "My show's
on" . . . "What is it?" . . . *Maverick*."

The voice of a deeply male cretinism started the show off
. . . "FROM HOLLYWOOD, THE ENTERTAINMENT CAPI-
TAL OF THE WORLD," he said, "BROUGHT TO YOU BY
WARNER BROTHERS."

"Did you hear that, Poppy? This is coming from Hollywood!" . . . "They say that every week, you idiot" . . .

The episode opens with Bret Maverick sitting at a poker
table . . . but right away there's something strange . . . this is
1959, years before color TV . . . and yet it's perfectly clear
. . . Maverick is blue! . . . his skin is an unmistakably dark
shade of blue . . . he nearly ignites the black-and-white world
around him . . .

Poppy says, "What the hell is the matter with this damned
TV set?" . . . "Is it going to explode?" . . . Poppy gets up to adjust the rabbit-ear antenna . . . no use . . . Blue Maverick
quivers but remains quite blue . . . Poppy changes the chan-

nel . . . Blue Maverick sits at a poker table on every channel!
. . . even Poppy's crusty, implacable and utterly changeless
facial expression—composed in equal parts of authority, self-
contempt, ennui and a sadness that knows not its own
name—even this monument to every-moment-the-same-as-
the-last-please! begins to quake under the implications . . .
Poppy frowns and, compelled by a weird force that he begins
to sense emanates from the Blue Maverick, returns to his
place on the couch . . . it is almost as if Blue Maverick is directing Poppy to sit and watch . . . it's about time . . . the old
meany hasn't been dealt with like this in years . . .

A weak, pusillanimous, pasty creature, a doctor perhaps,
comes through the swinging barroom door panicked . . . "Is
there a Mr. Maverick here?" he wants to know . . . Blue Maverick turns on him limpid cow eyes . . . immediately the
doctor's anxiety seems to melt . . . he seems drunk with the
color of a new joy . . . his eyes dart like birds . . . he is suddenly filled with an inexplicable ecstasy . . . a desire to repeat
the beloved name, Maverick . . .

At the table the players sing spontaneously . . . "Who is the
tall dark stranger there?" . . . instantly they know . . . "Maverick is his name" . . .

So captivated by his own joy is he that the doctor cannot
speak his message . . . Maverick reaches forth a single blue
finger and touches the spot on the doctor's forehead directly
between his eyes . . . immediately he is calmed . . . he speaks,
"Maverick, there's someone looking for you. He hates you. He
hates the lady called Luck who sits at your elbow. He's
lookin' to kill you. He is the demon John Wesley Burden-of-
the-Earth."

The camera holds fast on Blue Maverick's face, but it reveals no emotion save an oblique playfulness . . .

Blue Maverick smiles the spectacularly charming and boy-
ish smile for which he is paid $2,000 per week by television
tycoons and pushes the broad-brimmed hat back on his head
. . . his response is to sing, "I love a girl named Lila" . . . one of
his opponents interrupts stupidly, saying, "I call you, dark
stranger" . . . this savage man lays out a full house, aces over

kings . . . then Maverick lays out his impressive hand, a thousand suns risen all at once, a mass of splendor, shining on all sides, blazing fire . . .

"That sure beats me I guess," says the man . . . and Maverick smiles the smile of a god who is not remote and uncaring, but personal, attentive and accessible . . .

You can't imagine the effect this scene has on Poppy . . . I can't describe it . . . he looks blasted back against the sofa cushions . . . ideas are coming at him with the centrifugal force of a jet . . . thirty G's knock him silly . . . this is a guy who hasn't had a thought in years . . . the scales on his eyes have their own scales . . . the poor guy looks like the Upanishads have just been downloaded into his frontal lobe . . . he sees it all . . . worse yet, "his show" is just getting started . . . there's a commercial break . . .

A man who is perhaps Walt Disney's clone or automaton stands before a chalkboard wearing a white lab jacket . . . he carries a rubber-tipped pointer . . . "Hello, I'm Dr. Ronald Entirety. Our friends at Open Mouth Pharmaceuticals have asked me to speak to you tonight about a sensitive personal problem, a medical problem that affects both ourselves and our loved ones. Parasites."

Dr. Entirety moves to one side, revealing this image on a chalkboard:

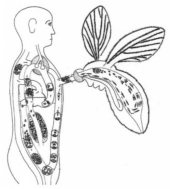

"Animal parasitism is a way of life" . . . reassuring smile
. . . "The parasite lives in or on another species, gaining its
livelihood at the other's expense" . . . Dr. Entirety strolls to
his right, out of the clinical environment and directly into a
domestic environment . . . one that looks every bit like the
typical American middle-class household of the 1950s
. . . it is Poppy's household except that it is polished . . . Dr.
Entirety sits in a replica of Poppy's couch and looks confidently into the camera . . . "Parasites live everywhere. Even
here in your own living room. They are in your carpet. Clinging to the follicles of your hair." He pulls a strand of his own
lank and greying locks. "In order to live in or on a host, a
parasite must evolve structures for adhering to it. Some develop tarsi for holding onto hair, others develop rigid hooks
which sink into flesh. In the most advanced types, as with the
trematodes, they have suckers that actually interlock with
our own fretted capillaries. When I return at the next commercial break, we'll see just how these creatures enter the
human host and what some of the consequences of this infes-
tation can be. But for now this is Dr. Ronald Entirety for our
friends at Open Mouth Pharmaceuticals saying, Fare thee
well."

Blue Maverick comes riding up over the crest of a hill on
the horse-demon Keshi . . . Keshi is gigantic, powerful, and
swift as the mind . . . he furrows the earth with his hooves,
crowds the sky with clouds, disperses the heavens with a
wave of his mane, and terrifies all who behold him . . .
Maverick has received a note from his old friend Ward
Harper, the owner of the Rocking H ranch and the man who
on one legendary morning discovered Maverick as an embryo
in his boot . . . with incredulous eyes Ward Harper beheld
Maverick, his mind confused and enraptured . . . he bent low
to praise the embryo which gestated in the cowboy's boot, and
the Maverick embryo whispered to him the story of his previous lives . . .

Ward Harper raised Maverick . . . cared for him from the day that Maverick emerged from his boot clinging like a marsupial to the rawhide fringe of Ward's chaps . . . In his youth, once, Maverick ate some dirt . . . Ward Harper was genuinely angry . . . "Did you eat dirt?" . . . "No, Ward Harper" . . . "I said, 'Did you eat dirt?' " . . . "No, sir, Ward Harper" . . . "Then open your mouth" . . . When Maverick opened his mouth, Ward Harper glimpsed the Universe, consisting of objects that move and objects that do not move, the ethereal dome, cardinal points, mountains, oceans, wind, fire, stars and even the mind itself . . . "Aha," said Ward Harper, "I knew it. Now why do you lie to me, boy?" . . . he grabbed little Maverick by the ear . . . "Don't you know that you can get sick eatin' that? . . . there's tiny critturs live in the dirt" . . .

In remorse, Maverick spit out the dirt . . . when it landed, it became the infinite and majestic Rocking H ranch . . .

But that was all long ago . . . now Ward Harper had different problems, bushwhackers . . . they finally succeeded . . . his string ran out . . . his body was found dry-gulched and back-shot on the road to Tucson . . . now was his son, Blue Maverick, come to repay the ancient debt to his Pappy, Ward Harper . . .

Eight centuries hadn't made any great changes in the ranch layout . . . the main ranch house was in need of paint . . . nearby was the cookhouse with the hand pump through which a young Maverick had once pumped an angry river demon, Pecos Ba-Gua, thus bringing an age of growth and prosperity to western Arizona . . . a long wooden bench lined with wash basins was under the porch awning . . . in the corral, the young cows ran to the rail at Maverick's approach and wept from their big round eyes calling his name . . . Moooverick . . .

Blue Maverick rode directly to the main ranch house and hitched Keshi to the rail in front . . . just before entering the house, he looked up for the familiar plume of smoke which for eight hundred years had curled from the chimney . . . but the chimney was cold . . . Maverick entered without knocking and whistled the tune to "I love a girl named Lila" . . .

The room Maverick entered was a man's room . . . there were animal heads on the wall—antelopes, mountain goats and buffalo . . . hides covered everything . . . rifles hung in the few empty spots, Sharps and Remingtons . . . Maverick began to understand how things had gone wrong . . . one by one,] visited each buffalo and antelope, stroking its head, kissii its brow and feeling for the force of a lost life in each sile horn . . . tears came to the glass eyes of each beast . . .

Could his Pappy, honored Ward Harper, have gone so wrong? . . . Ward Harper had taken him in and taught him many things . . . it was Ward Harper who had said to him, "Work is all right for killing time, but it's a shaky way to make a living" . . . these words were now etched into temple walls in the holy city of Amarillo . . . for these reasons, Maverick felt he owed Ward Harper a boundless debt, and he was here now to pay it . . . but these deaths hung on the wall of a room meant for life . . . it could not be a good sign . . .

Then a voice came from a back room . . . "Who's there? Just a minute" . . . but when the person belonging to this voice entered the room, she was no young woman, surely not his sister Lila, but someone terribly old, superannuated in fact . . . she wore curlers in her hair that hadn't been removed in several decades, as if she'd been stood up at the high-school prom and left in these curlers while her "date" vomited Southern Comfort on some other girl's front porch . . . she wore a tattered robe, open indecently in the front . . . and she carried a rifle which she leveled at Blue Maverick's heart . . . could this be the little eleven-year-old barefooted girl in pigtails and peeling sunburn that Maverick remembered? . . . could a mere eight centuries have been so harsh on her? . . .

"Lila? Sister?" he asked, his heart breaking.

When she saw it was Maverick, she put down the rifle . . . "Ah, Maverick, returned too late after all these years" . . . she walked slowly toward him now, changing as she approached, opening her robe and revealing breasts that were in fact the heavy breasts of a young woman . . . she raised them in her hands . . . Lila's face grew more youthful, a face of charming smiles and sidelong glances . . . "I've waited here for you, brother, for so long . . . please drink" . . . and she lifted her breasts toward his mouth, the milk already spilling from his nipples and running in pearly streams down her stomach . . .

"Drink . . ."

"**HELLO AGAIN**. Dr. Entirety from Open Mouth Pharmaceuticals, and I'm here tonight to talk to you about parasites.

"What is a parasite? Well, it may be an organism that helps you, like the bacteria in your intestinal tract, or it may be an organism that hurts you, like the mad parameceum that will swim to your brain and set up there a housekeeping not in the least neighborly. But whether friend or foe, these bugs will eventually eat you. Let me put it this way, there are things out there, with their own genetic story to tell, that wish to inhabit you and live your life for you.

"But let's take a moment to look at some of the nastier varieties we humans might encounter."

"This is our little antagonist *Trypanosoma cruzi*. It is pathogenic to humans.

"How do we come in contact with this little cutie? Well, I'm sorry to tell you this, but on occasion humans do things that perhaps they oughtn't. Oh not you, my friends, and probably not anyone you know, but there are people out there who seem clean but they are not.

"And what, you might like to know, are some of the things that unclean people do? I will tell you bluntly: contaminated feces come in contact with the mucus membrane of the lips or eyes. Don't ask me how. It is simply a medical fact. Or the disease is transmitted by the thoughtless members of the reduviid bug family. A case in point: while feeding on a vertebrate, the reduviid habitually defecates, voiding feces that contain numerous metacyclic trypanosomes like the *cruzi*. The fecal matter enters the skin through punctures made by the biting of the bug.

"Finally, venereal equations of an unspeakable nature are not out of the question. Yes, to answer the question that you are all asking out there, the venereal equations can and do involve feces and certainly in statistically significant numbers even the reduviid bug himself.

"Not a nice thing to contemplate, I agree.

"Believe me, there is more to know of this character, the parasite. At the next commercial break I would like to speak to you of the unsuspected connection we have to the gut of the land snail.

"Until then, I am Dr. Ronald Entirety, speaking for your friends at Open Mouth Pharmaceuticals, saying, Until that fateful day!"

Blue Maverick, however, was quite aware that this was not really his sister Lila . . . and he sensed that her breasts flowed not with milk, but with a deadly poison distilled in fact from the horns of a million murdered buffalo . . . Maverick closed his eyes and allowed the beautiful woman to take him on her lap as if he were her infant . . . but when she gave him her tit, Blue Maverick squeezed it between his powerful hands . . . "Whoa, honey, that's a little rough," she said . . . "Simmer down. You know, that can hurt a girl. That's sensitive business in your mitts there. Owee. OWWWEEEE!" . . . then Maverick sucked the tit and along with it her life . . . his seductress grimaced as if a creature with small tooth-like projections of the family Dictyocaulus filaria were dragging her lungs up and out through her gaping mouth . . . being crushed in all of her vital parts, she cried out for him to let go, but Maverick would not let go his grip . . . her body was drenched in perspiration, and her hands and feet lashed about convulsively . . . "I mean it, baby doll, this is not quality time for me, this is not a life-enhancing experience" . . . still

Maverick persisted in his squeezing and sucking until she dropped dead . . . only a thin string of her poisonous milk drooped from his lips and then, with a flip, rose and entered his nose . . . but Blue Maverick did not have time to consider the meaning or portent of this strange milk . . . he had to find his own Lila . . .

He walked to the back room, the same room from which the demonic woman had come, and there was his lovely sister Lila, just putting the finishing touches on a rawhide vest with the name MAVERICK blazoned in red rhinestones on the back . . . for hers was a pure and endless devotion . . .

As Maverick looked upon her, he was struck through with passion . . . dark blue in appearance and extremely handsome, Maverick had the same effect upon her . . . instantly, Lila, lovely Lila, dropped her fancywork and revealed to Maverick—behind her own calico skirt printed with designs of a white church and a red schoolhouse—her great loins and buttocks, both wonderfully strong . . . it was between these thighs that Visnu had placed the cosmos, like a dense walnut that, when cracked, exploded with its infinite light . . .

Maverick then committed with his sister Lila, there on the bare dirt floor of that rancher's home, the eight kinds of sexual intercourse (adverse, etc.), systematically assailing her with teeth, nails, hands and lips . . . he kissed her in eight mysterious ways consistent with the doctrines of sexual science and delightful to the ladies . . .

Done, Maverick rose from the floor and said, "Oh Visnu, shit, I'm some dude! I could eat the world, no problem. Give it to me, I'm ready. I'll open my mouth for you. You can place it on the tip of my tongue like a breath mint."

Lila could not guess it at the moment, but this filial conjuncture had wrought a change in beloved Maverick . . . certain critical synapses had begun simmering in a cerebral brine . . . Lila would have cause to remember this moment in days to come . . . she would recognize it in the diagnostic manual under the heading, "initiating episode" . . . do not be surprised at this . . . we are always astonished to learn of such-a-one's mental illness . . . "he seemed just fine to me"

. . . "I saw him last week, happy as a clam" . . . but even our gods hide flaw, damage, genetic error . . . yes, even our gods are "cracked" or there is no explaining this world . . .

Dr. Entirety is standing behind a white enameled table surrounded by the trappings of science . . . Bunsen burners, test tubes, microscopes, centrifuges, voltage meters, alligator clips for the testicles . . . he has before him a tray of snails, moving back and forth with the best show of panic a snail can muster . . . he holds one of the snails in his left hand while running, with scientific detachment, what appears to be a glass pipette deep into the snail's cavity . . . a bit of drooling snail matter actually runs down the pipette and then down Dr. Entirety's fingers . . . with a shudder of disgust, Entirety drops both pipette and snail . . . the pipette shatters on the countertop . . . the snail lands with a nauseating crunch among his brethren snails multiplying their frenzy, giving objective content to their snail-dread . . .

"Hello, again," Entirety says, wiping his hands on his smock . . .

"You probably don't think of yourself as much in contact with the snail, do you? The connection probably seems to you distant and unlikely. Well, what if I told you that the pulmonate land snail *(anguispira alternata)* is an enemy, not only to your garden, but to you. For he carries a malevolent essence in his gut. His scientific name says it all: *anguispira alternata.* He is our anguish breathing Other. Skeptical? Well, look here."

"Snails frequently gather together with aquatic organisms such as arthropods and amphibians. The infective *metacercariae* (or "Voodoo mask" parasite) lurks among them. Fully embryonated eggs enclosed in thick, impervious shells are passed in the feces of the definitive host. A hatching occurs in the gut of the land snail. *Cercariae,* released in the air chambers of the snail, provoke an excessive secretion of mucus which surrounds them in an environment which clinicians call 'slimeballs'. These slimeballs are discharged into the vegetation or soil where they can wait protected in slime for the inevitable arrival of a human host.

"Not to put too fine a point on it, the *metacercariae* are lapped up from the fronds of unwashed vegetables. Or they are ingested along with clumps of soil. Or the *cercariae* (a.k.a. the-bug-our-death) enter the openings of the ureter. How does this happen! How does the human organ of micturition and regeneration, male or female, come in contact with the slime trail of the garden snail? We do not know. We cannot speculate. But it is a scientific fact.

"Things then accumulate in the blood. Parasitemia. Lymph nodes, liver and spleen become enlarged. The patient develops a fever. The parasites migrate to and accumulate in the central nervous system. They invade the brain. Are you understanding this important point? The disease terminates with a headache and death.

"This sort of thing is not acceptable to the good folks at Open Mouth Pharmaceuticals. They are not amused. The 'snail connection' is not evidence of a quaint regional custom. This is not something to be protected and preserved by a misguided Smithsonian. It is evidence of humans in league with forces bent upon our destruction."

Dr. Entirety picks up another snail and examines it closely . . . a tiny spermy ball of slime appears beneath the snail . . . quickly, Dr. Entirety's expression changes from one of distant disinterest to horror and personal urgency . . . he looks directly into the camera and begins screaming, "Stop it! Do you hear me? Stop it, stop it, stop it! It's intolerable! You are a foul people! Most foul! Disgusting! You disgust me!"

Fade to black . . . a voice-over suggests: "Dr. Entirety will return with a final comment from the good people at Open Mouth Pharmaceuticals after this dramatic interlude."

Maverick and Lila began restoring the Rocking H to a place meant for life . . . they removed the hides from the floor and furniture, sweetly lifted the animal heads from the walls and created an enormous consecrated pyre in the yard . . . the demon that Maverick had sucked dry, it turned out, was made of paraffin . . . chopping her body and mixing it with fragrant sandalwood, they fueled the fire which would allow the slaughtered beasts, and even the demon herself, to enter the great Wringer, out of which they might return as something superior . . . clearly, they'd earned it . . . perhaps they would return as cowboys . . . sure enough, just as the flames began leaping toward the celestial dome, a chorus of cowboys appeared, their necks draped with colorful bandanas . . . they began to sing an ancient hymn:

I love a girl named Lila,
She's nicer than my dog,
And when I think of Lila,
My feet begin to clog.

They stomp the ground in bliss,
Worshipping this miss,
And begging for a kiss,
Say, "What a girl, this Lila!"

Oh Lila, lovely Lila,
Our heads go all agog,
Oh skinny, juicy Lila,
Nicer than my dog.

The ceremony done, the cowboys threw their Stetson hats in the air, harumphing in cowboy happiness and shooting their guns in admiration at the stars . . . then they turned to their bunkhouse . . . they set to work in an instant and before the afternoon was over the roof was patched, the siding freshly painted, the floors scrubbed and the cowboy beds made . . . at night, they lined up in their flannel pajamas with the bucking broncos on them . . . Maverick shook their hands and Lila kissed their cheeks . . .

Then Maverick and Lila sat down so that she could tell him the whole story . . . it was long and sad, and often tears came to Maverick's eyes to think of his Pappy's suffering . . . the Rocking H was in debt . . . $50,000 . . . the mortgage was due in five days . . . a local financier had bought the loan from the bank . . . he meant to take over and throw Lila and all her many cowboy devotees off the land . . . his name was John Wesley Burden-of-the-Earth . . . and he was no one to fool with . . . for he was all business . . . and, as if this weren't bad enough, he was a dead shot, the fastest gun in the West . . . and thus has it ever been with financiers . . .

To pay off the original mortgage, Lila herself had gone out and rounded up two thousand steer and on her little dappled roan drove them to Kansas City . . . this should have provided plenty of money to pay off the mortgage, but Burden-of-the-Earth had arranged a stage robbery, seized the money chest, and with that same money bought the Rocking H mortgage for himself . . . this irony made him chuckle . . . to ensure that Lila executed no more one-woman cattle drives, he placed his own sister, a demon named Budding Beauty Vanity, as her governess . . . this had all happened within the last two hundred years . . .

But Blue Maverick's arrival had messed up their little game . . . or at least complicated it . . . on the other hand, the death of Burden-of-the-Earth's sister, Budding Beauty Vanity, had made Burden very cross . . . what's worse, Burden's henchmen laughed behind his back about the lurid means of her death . . . at night, lying sleepless in bed, Burden saw Blue Maverick with his teeth sunk in his sister's tit, sucking her dry . . . it was a tit, in fact, that Burden-of-the-Earth himself had sucked, her poison for him his life's blood . . . he was determined to destroy Maverick . . . he had legitimacy, the rule of law, on his side . . . therefore he summoned the sheriff, Mr. Machine, to arrest Maverick for suspicion of murder in the death of his sister . . .

But it was no easy thing to locate Maverick during this period . . . oh, one might have hoped, one surely would have expected, that he would settle down to tending the ranch, recovering its fortune, paying off the mortgage, siring blue avatars in his comely sister . . . but the elation of returning home after eight hundred years, the ecstasy of carnal relations with Lila on their father's dirt floor, these facts seem to have made Blue Maverick a bit "tetched," as we used to say . . . he was experiencing an excess of optimism . . . he was "on top of the world" in the naughty sense . . . he was caught in the play of a manic gloom and glee between which he careened like a battered shuttlecock . . . Lila was very worried . . .

For example, one evening Maverick returned home and announced that he was going back to school . . . he was an outstanding student, but for unfathomable reasons he decided that he would do secretarial work rather than go on to college . . . he developed many avocational interests including ballet, reading and languages . . . soon Lila and the worshipful cowpokes noticed that Maverick was going out every night . . . he began dating men, attending church meetings, language classes and dances . . . he got a job at a local insurance agency where his seductiveness resulted in his going to bed with two of the available married men . . . he burst into tears on occasion and told risqué jokes . . . he became talkative and restless, stopped eating, and didn't seem to need any sleep . . . he began to talk about being in contact with God, which frankly was news to no one, but also expressed a conviction that it was God's wish that he give himself sexually to all who needed him . . . there was no news in this either . . .

When it was suggested by Lila that he was "going too fast" and "doing too much in life," he became quite angry . . . "Lila," he shouted, "I am a god! I am one of Visnu's chosen! Gods do not suffer from excessively busy work schedules!" . . . convinced by his own irreproachable logic, he became so enraged that he killed one of the cowboys—who had come along with Lila for moral support—by reaching in through his mouth and pulling him inside out . . . this crisis was easily, but guiltily, papered over, for no one, not the authorities and not even the cowboys themselves, were really quite sure about just

exactly how many cowboys there were out at the Rocking
H . . .

And, it should go without saying, there was much of gambling . . . Maverick became legendary for his gambling . . .
poker, horses, pitching nickels, any gambit was worthy of his
attention . . . on one day alone he won all of Madagascar . . . in
fact, he lost every hand but the last that night in perfect good
humor . . . then, at the stroke of twelve, he suggested that
they play for their respective properties . . . he put up his sister Lila . . . he showed his skeptical opponents convincing
Polaroids that demonstrated that in fact Lila's buttocks were
the equivalent of the rolling foothills of the fertile Loire Val-
ley . . . in an inspired tactic, he insisted that they play a
single hand of "Indian" poker, winner take all . . . the ludi-
crous seven of diamonds that he pressed to his forehead
caused his gaming companions to laugh and wager with impunity . . . you can imagine their chagrin when between the
four of them they could manage only a five of clubs . . . well,
he left the house that night with the deeds not only to Madagascar but to large tracts of Louisiana, the Russian steppes
and a particularly rich fishing pond in rural Iowa . . .

As any gambler knows, however, a hot streak is only a cold
streak waiting to happen . . . within a week, he returned
home not merely calmer but despondent . . . he sat in his
room and could not be convinced to speak . . . the news of his
losses trickled in slowly . . . at first, he paid off his debts by
liquidating his assets . . . he clear-cut his rain forest holdings, relocated the indigenous tribe (which in any case was
extinct within a few years from AIDS and the exotic Kansas
City flu), slaughtered the two hundred thousand dwarf deer
that lived there, then sold the mineral rights to a strip-min-
ing company . . . but it soon became clear that these resources
would not stanch the flow . . . an affidavit from the International Bankers Confidence Fund demonstrated compellingly
that Lila was now the property of a transnational banking
consortium with headquarters in Berne . . . and the lovely
singing cowboys were the property of a Mister Phookeet who
owned a nightclub called Lipstick in the Patpong district of

Bangkok . . . dutifully, they went off and, frankly, have never been heard from again . . . occasionally, a tourist will return with a strange story of meeting little Eurasian boys in Stetson hats on the beaches of the Gulf of Thailand where they perform lewd acts with their lips in return, they insist, for "silver dollars" . . . a devastating devotion indeed . . .

Lila was crushed by these turns in fate . . . "Maverick, will I really have to go? Are you sure this is legal?" . . . Maverick showed no emotion . . . perhaps he felt guilty, perhaps this was the final shock that would allow him to change his ways, but he showed no sign of it . . . still, there was nothing unclear in his thinking . . . he knew the answer to her question precisely . . . "I'm afraid, my love, that for the International Bankers Confidence Fund there are few issues of law that can impinge upon its great transnational will . . . of course you will have to go . . . of course you will do as they bid . . . of course it will not be pleasant . . . but" . . . he grew suddenly confident . . . "my luck is bound to change . . . I can feel it . . . it rises in me like a green fuse . . . I will play a single hand of five-card draw with the executive director in charge of foreign holdings . . . I will win" . . . "But what will you wager? You've lost everything" . . . "My virility if it is necessary . . . my very blueness" . . . an image of Maverick's blue penis against the green felt of the card table came to Lila's suffering mind and she shuddered . . .

Before these awful ideas could come to a head, fate intervened . . . it was an inconsequential trip into town . . . Maverick was just getting down out of the buckboard with Miss Lila at his side when Sheriff Machine called out to him . . . "Maverick, I'm going to have to ask you for your gun, son" . . . Sheriff Machine's body was a transparent, fun, take-apart body . . . you could see all of his internal gears . . . when he walked his mouth opened and closed rhythmically as if he were saying something very stupid over and over again . . . something like, "Goobers, goobers, goobers" . . . he was a potent idiot . . . but since Sheriff Machine had no functional elbows, he was notoriously slow on the draw . . . he had been shot dead a hundred times by every drunk no-good in the territory . . .

133

they used him for target practice as if he were no more than a tin can . . . in short, even the only occasionally omnipotent Maverick could take him in a moment . . .

And he was about to when, to his left, John Wesley Burden-of-the-Earth appeared, packing hardware . . . "What's he doing here, Sheriff?" . . . "Oh, he's properly deputized, don't you worry about that" . . . "Well, then I guess it's just you and me, Burden-of-the-Earth" . . . "Yep" . . . "Any time you're ready" . . . "Show me what you got, cowpoke" . . .

The invitation to show the gathered townsfolk what he had was welcome to Blue Maverick . . . he felt suddenly euphoric, capable of anything . . . good golly, Visnu, he was top of the tops . . . then thirty of Burden's thugs appeared from behind every wagon, horse, and corner in the square . . . he was outnumbered and without hope . . . but this only made the challenge and the opportunity for glory seem the greater to him . . . he smiled broadly . . .

Lila screamed, "Maverick, you're crazy! Don't do this! It can't be done! They'll kill you!" . . . but he moved forward, hands ready . . . the fact that he had less than one-quarter of the bullets, never mind the hand speed, necessary for this feat seemed curiously beside the point to him . . .

"Maverick," pleaded Lila, "how many times does six bullets go into thirty men? Do you remember the rules for long division? Let me show you in the dirt with this stick" . . .

John Wesley Burden-of-the-Earth seemed amused . . . "Maverick, why this folly? Do you love the gamble so much that you wish to die for it?" . . .

This was an interesting question he'd been asked . . . Maverick considered what it would mean to answer it properly . . . he pondered . . . he used the instant as if it were twenty years of solitude in the mountains, and he answered frankly if not wisely . . .

"For me, John Wesley Burden-of-the-Earth, gambling is a question posed to Fate: Am I loved?"

Burden-of-the-Earth was reasonably perplexed . . . "But my dear Maverick . . . you have posed this question to Fate a thousand times even in the last month."

"Yes," replied Maverick, his blueness surging and radiant, "I want to be sure."

"Sure! Sure of what, my boy? Sometimes the answer to your question has been yes, sometimes no, sometimes maybe . . . what does that tell you about the quality of the question itself? . . . perhaps you ask the wrong question" . . .

Maverick was shaken . . . it hadn't occurred to him that there might be something wrong with the question itself . . . but that put into doubt every premise of his life . . . Burden didn't need to shoot poor Maverick, he had flung him into the abyss with a question . . . Maverick had been tossed out toward the most distant, inhuman stellar range where his sleeve had caught on a star's point . . . he felt he hung there, alone and wretched . . . suddenly the sun on that little western town square throbbed through Maverick's eyeball to his brain with a hot sense of heaviness and pain . . . and he said . . .

"You are right. I am not loved."

"For goodness sake, Maverick, that's not what I meant," groaned John Wesley. "Besides, it's perfectly obvious even to people, like myself, bent upon your destruction that the courteous Lila here loves you, even if her love is in questionable taste and perhaps evidence of your mutually damaged genetic past" . . .

"That's true, dearest," pled Lila, "you are loved . . . I love you!"

"Your love does not count," Maverick sneered . . .

Even Burden-of-the-Earth was amazed at this reply . . . "Young man, why in the world not?"

These words of care from one who was his sworn enemy threw Maverick into a rage . . . "Because, as you yourself say, you stupid, she is just my sister! She's just my stupid sister!" . . . Maverick was crying . . . he struggled to remove his gun but couldn't seem to get it out . . . he wanted to shoot someone . . . but he couldn't get his gun out of the holster . . . it was stuck . . . could somebody help him? . . . Burden crossed his arms and smiled sadly . . . "Goodness, goodness" . . . "I'm going to kill you!" screamed Maverick, his voice climbing registers . . .

Then Burden-of-the-Earth did something quite amazing
. . . he lifted his right hand and, cocking his thumb, pointed
his finger dead at Maverick's head . . . right between the eyes
. . . Maverick froze and stared . . . there was a dense quiet
. . . would he shoot? . . .

"Bang," said John Wesley Burden-of-the-Earth . . .

Maverick shuddered, his knees buckling . . .

Then everyone broke out in laughter . . . all the simple grey
townsfolk . . . they clapped him on the back . . . town drunks
and mooncalfs guffawed in his face . . . local humor, simple-
tons, grinned and ran their sooty fingers across their throats
. . . *kaput!* . . . what a clown, what a feeb, what a joke, the
great Maverick, a poltroon, a slicker, a mere tinhorn . . .

Maverick stood there, broken, as the townspeople moved
away in their devastating mirth . . . Lila came to his side . . .
she put her handkerchief to his nose . . . "Blow," she said . . .
"Come on, blow . . . Your nose is running" . . . Maverick blew
. . . as if it were written somewhere, as if the runny tale of a
blown nose were tea leaves in which the future could be read,
they both looked into the handkerchief . . . a tiny, milk-white
worm wriggled against the cotton . . .

Finally, the awful truth . . . Maverick was tainted . . . Maverick was occupied, infested, his brain crawling with an over-
flowing alien life like the hemispheres of an infected walnut
. . . whether it was the pulsing soil he ate as a child or the
contaminated milk of Budding Beauty Vanity, this made
little difference . . . he had a bad brain . . . Lila looked into her
beloved brother's eyes and saw not the divine radiance of earlier days but the shadows of worms who moved from lobe to
lobe . . .

The end

A live shot of Dr. Entirety's laboratory . . . he is not there
. . . one sees only his counter with the large white-enameled

tray in which are the snails . . . they now crawl freely . . . they circle the lip of the tray and wander the countertop itself, inching aimlessly, leaving behind their luminous, infected trails . . . a few have fallen to the tile floor, crushing their shells . . . others have successfully descended the legs of the counter and are moving about the floor of the lab . . .

But there is apparently no human in control here . . . where is Dr. Entirety? . . . is this a mistake? . . . embarrassing mistakes happened frequently enough in the early days of TV . . . is this simply the wrong set? . . . has the wrong switch been thrown? . . . when will this error be realized? . . . worse yet, this is no avant-garde underground film, this is expensive, commercially ripe prime time, and this is a horror . . . the camera stares at the slow fury of the snails for ten consecutive hours before this grim technical difficulty ends . . . and it ends only when very gradually a moist shadow quietly eclipses the camera lens . . .

"**You two goombahs!**" Mommy shouts . . . "What in the world are you two doin'?"

Poppy and the boy stare at a moist, tubercular patch on the TV screen . . . Mommy yanks on the venetian blind cord . . . it is morning . . . the blinds go rattling towards the ceiling with an explosion of dust . . . but on the brilliant morning light, the dust is hovering diamonds . . .

"Good Lord, get some fresh air . . . it stinks in here . . . that TV will be the death of you two . . . come on, breakfast is almost ready . . . honey? coffee! . . . Sonny? Maypo!" . . .

Poppy and the boy look at each other for what seems the first time in centuries . . . there are tears in the boy's eyes . . . Poppy, too, feels confused and saddened, but he also feels pity for the boy's fear and so he gets up from the couch, takes the boy by the hand, and leads him out the front door . . . they sit together on the tiny concrete stoop and Poppy puts an arm around the boy's slumping shoulder . . .

"Poppy, that show scared me. What was it about?"

"It was scary to me, too, Butch. And I don't know what it was about. But remember, that's all just life-on-TV. That's not real life."

The boy looks up at this father, the huge round eyes of youth brimming with enormous tears . . . his father's eyes brimming with the enormity of his lie . . .

"Tell you what," says Poppy, "Whaddaya say you and me play a little catch before breakfast?"

"What kind of catch?"

"Football catch."

"You sure Mom won't be mad?"

"Nah, she'll understand."

"Okay, then."

"Now where is that football? Didn't I see it underneath the lawn mower? And where would the pump be?"

Poppy goes off in search of the football, but the boy remains on the stoop, staring in that splendid mix of confusion and pain that makes youth memorable . . . then, slowly, an idea begins to wriggle across his face . . . the flesh of his face seems to crawl with concept . . . he raises his right hand and points his index finger . . . he cocks his thumb back . . . he points in the air . . . he feels the rumble of a pure power rise from his bowels . . . pkeew . . . he points at a bush . . . PKEEW . . . Poochie comes stumbling out from behind the corner of the house and pauses, naked, exposed, uncertain . . . Poochie wonders, What's he doing outside? . . . the two, boy and dog, lock stares for a moment, then the boy says, "Hold it right there, Poochie" . . . the grim creature freezes, a look of intense doggy anxiety in its eyes . . . the boy points his finger right between the dog's eyes . . . "Freeze or you're a dead dog" . . . Poochie can't get more frozen . . . "Pity me," he seems to say . . . "I just want to live my miserable doggy existence, same as you" . . . the boy smiles . . . "Good boy, Poochie. But you're a dead dog anyway" . . . PKEEW, PKEEW, PKEEW . . . Poochie shudders . . . if something furry can go white, he goes white . . . "Gotcha! You're dead, Poochie! You're dead!" . . . he's howling, laughing, this goofy kid, this wormy apple . . . "You're dead, Poochie! Aha ha! . . . I really shot you! HA HA HA HA HA HA HA!"

Poochie wobbles, waddling slowly in reverse on his arthritic dog legs and returns to his smelly backyard paradise . . .

Poppy returns wiping cobwebs and motor oil from a half-inflated football . . . "Found it! Here we go! I'm Y. A. Tittle. Who the hell are *you?*"

"R. C. Owens."

"Go deep, R. C.!"

Poppy disappears into the front yard, tossing the ball to himself in little comical downfield spirals . . .

The boy stands slowly, looking after his father . . . then he notices something . . . something high in his peripheral vision . . . it's a color, a vivid color . . . it's intense, shocking, spreading behind the tormented branches of a sycamore tree . . . it's blue . . . the color blue . . . he can't recall ever seeing it before . . . he could be mistaken, but it would appear that the entire sky is the color blue.

Now, for most people, the sky's blueness is a given (and, for all that, is therefore less than fully blue) . . . but for the boy emerging for the first time from his grey, repeatable night . . . emerging from his stinking pre-fab mousehole, this was a new and exhilarating discovery . . . and you will forgive him if he assumed, with an excess of childish, poetic enthusiasm, that it was again Maverick intruding on a black-and-white world . . . it was Maverick that he saw high behind the sycamores . . . he bent, brooding, over the world with his warm blue breast and—ah!—his bright laughing eyes.

SATURDAY NIGHT AT THE MOVIES

Marshmallows. I see the marshmallows. They fling themselves above me, high flyin'. I watch them with a dulled absorption.

Patting. Something is patting my face. A gentle rain of gentle pats. On my nose, cheeks and mouth.

Then God speaks. God is the atmosphere in which marshmallows fling themselves toward the heavens. And God is the moral climate in which one's face is patted. But God is also capable of infusing his world with voice.

God can say: "Butch, what in the hell are you doing?"

My father-who-art-on-the-couch, hallowed be thy Life-on-TV. He hath risen like Christ from the tomb; he is a lily sprouting like a mushroom from the humid cushions of the davenport. He has lifted himself from recumbancy, as if someone had asked the famous reclining Buddha for a dance.

So I'm looking straight up out of my own sympathetic grave. My father is on his knees looking back over the edge of the chesterfield, as if over the edge of his own coffin. His arms rest on the edge, God brooding over his world, wondering, "Why did I make THAT?" I lie below him, on the floor, flat on my back, dozens of Kraft miniature marshmallows littered around my head like spent shrapnel.

"I'm not doin' nothin', Dad."

"No, Son, that's not nothin'. I can only wish you were doin' nothin'. Nothin' would be a big step up from this. Compared to this, nothin' gets your name on a banner high up in the rafters of the high-school gymnasium. So, no, it's not nothin'. It's the quality of the *somethin'* that I'm wondering about."

I scrunch my face searching for a way of expressing my sense of hopeless bewilderment.

"No, Son, let me tell you what you're doin'. You're throwing marshmallows up in the air and letting them land on your face. Can you give me the rhyme and reason for this?"

I can feel my eyebrows, nose and mouth shudder and convulse. What have I meant?

God clucks his tongue. "You just don't make sense."

He continues. "Now let's take a look at what your hands are doing."

My hands. Again. Doing things. Why were boys supposed to be responsible for what their little hands did? It wasn't fair. I looked over at my right hand, fearing the worst. Marshmallows had, over a period of tremendous geological change, of the complete collapse of one climate empire after another, marshmallows had, I may now safely reveal, now that it is too late and no amount of filtering, recycling and federal intervention will make the least difference, marshmallows had with the persistent force that is nature's own, melted down between my fingers, dripped through like stalactites or mites, making thus a most guilty and sticky clotted cream.

"Not that hand. The other hand."

Oh, that hand was an innocent hand! Let me look then for the true culprit, mister left hand, mister sneaky sinister. But I couldn't find it.

"Where is it, Dad?"

"Where's what?"

"My other hand."

"Where's your other hand? You can't find your own hand? Jesus! Send out a fucking search party! Call the FBI! He can't find his own goddamned hand!"

He waited. I did nothing. Then with a mocking look of exasperation he held his own left hand out as if to show me how it was done. With his extended left hand he formed a pistol. With the pistol he touched his temple.

I turned my head to the left and was suddenly looking right down the barrel. I could see the whorling bore of the gun, so much like a fingerprint.

Using my sodden right hand, I gently and compassionately lowered my rigid left, just praying that it was no hair-trigger affair. A tragedy averted.

Then Dad turned and sat back down on the davenport. Over the edge I could just see his hand gesture as though he was trying to throw a curveball, which I took to mean I should come sit with him.

Now this may all seem like just another evening in your average, damaged middle-class household. Not so! Remember, my father had not spoken to me since I was an infant. This was like wanting to know who had killed your best friend and then being given the extraordinary opportunity to ask questions of the victim himself.

I got up from behind the couch, wiping my fingers on my blue jeans, and sat next to my father. I kept my hands on my lap where I could keep an eye on them. Before us, like a dumb show, were my sisters. Winny moved to-and-fro before the TV like a deranged shuttle. Janey stood to the right, her mouth open like an orator's. A deep "Oh" emerged from her.

My father considered them. "Jesus Christ. As if you weren't bad enough. What in the world are your sisters doing?"

"I don't know."

"Are they always like this?"

"Maybe."

"What do you know?"

"I don't know."

At this point, of course, anybody's fatherly despair would be in order. But at just that moment I realized what a once-in-a-lifetime opportunity stood before me. I was speaking with my father. We were having a chat. I could ask him a question if I dared. I could ask him, what happened? Who dunnit? Were there witnesses? Where might my mighty revenge focus its awful energy? Time became mythic.

"Dad."

"Yes, Son."

"Can I ask you a question?"

"Sure."

"Are you happy?"

"Am I happy?"

"Yeah."

"Yes, I'm a very happy person."

"You are?"

"Of course."

"How do you know?"

"I'm happy because I just am. I have your mother and I have you kids and we have Poochie and the house and nice things like the TV."

"Dad, why do you watch TV every night?"

"I like the TV, Son. I enjoy it. It's very entertaining."

"You watch TV because it's entertaining?"

"That's right."

"Oh."

(Pause)

"Dad, why don't you talk to me or Winny or Janey?"

"I don't have anything to say to you. It's nothing personal. If I had something to say, I'd say it."

"Well, why don't you have something to say?"

"Like what?"

"Like anything."

"Like now?"

"I guess so. Yeah. We're talking now. Why can't we always do this?"

"This is different because we're not really talking, we're talking about talking."

"Oh."

(Pause)

"Dad, why do you drink?"

"Drink?"

"You always drink that stuff that Mom calls booze. That Old Crow booze."

"Well, again, it's nothing mysterious. I just like to drink."

"You like to drink?"

"Yes. It makes me feel good. I enjoy it. It's part of what makes being an adult fun. When you grow up, you'll like to drink too. Drinking is like a good friend."

"Oh."

"So you see, Son, I'm happy because I have a nice TV to

watch and drinks to drink. And that's all there is to it."

"Oh."

"Say, hey, listen, let's cut all this jabber and watch a movie. What do you say? It's Saturday night and there's a movie on. One of my favorites."

"What's the name of it?"

"*The Third Man.*"

"What about Winny and Janey?"

"Leave them be. This movie's for you and me. Except Winny keeps getting in the way."

Dad gets up and moves Winny to one side. She continues to pace robot-like but out of our view.

"You make a better door than you do a window, Winny," he says.

"Son, have I ever told you about my experiences in post-war Vienna, when I was with the Allied Army of Occupation?"

Not a damned word.

"I never knew the old Vienna before the war, with its Strauss music, its glamour and easy charm—Constantinople suited me better."

"Constantiwhat?"

"Well, I had many fine adventures and I'm gonna tell you every one of them. But when Carol Reed and Orson Welles made this movie in Vienna back in 1948, they put me in it!"

"You're in this movie?"

"Bet your bottom dollar!"

"Who are you?"

"What makes you think I'm a who?"

"What else could you be?"

"Maybe I'm a building or a bridge."

"You're a bridge in this movie?"

"I'm kidding you, Son. Why don't you just watch and tell me if you think someone or something is me."

A black-and-white shadowy world begins to emerge. It is the world of my parents, the world before I was born.

A brisk cosmopolitan narrator speaks: "*Vienna doesn't look any worse than a lot of other European cities, bombed about a bit . . . Oh wait, I was going to tell you . . . about Holly Martins from America . . ."*

"Dad, you were from America!"

"Sure was."

"Well, is that you? Holly Martins?"

"Don't talk. Watch the movie, Son."

"He came all the way here to visit a friend of his. The name was Lime, Harry Lime."

Opening Credits: A striated field, like a ruled pad of paper, made of the strings of a zither. Immediately the strings begin to vibrate, resonate with their great theme. Harry Lime. Harry Lime! Everything in this world evokes him while he remains persistently hidden. But this zither, our first "authenticity" in a movie that is often like a documentary of Cold War Vienna, has its own peculiarities. Are zithers truly a Germanic instrument? Is this sunny sound not more appropriate to the Mediterranean? The Greek *kithara*. Think of Vienna, whose grim streets are like claustrophobic canyons. Its severe facades always seem just a degree away from toppling. Why is this music here? It plays a tune that is lilting in pure, deranged contradiction to its context. It is the joie-de-vivre-unto-death. It is possessed, demoniacal, happy-go-lucky, a real self-motivator, fatal, unhinged, a good chap, funny, misplaced, grimy, suicidal, scandalous, merry, jocund, fleeting, ditty-like, of a certain airiness, depraved, condemned, merciless, unrepentant, and in general a scandal. When *The Third Man* played on TV, during my childhood, there was no escaping this zither which seemed to drench the house in human tears. It is the most perfect and perfectly inappropriate music in the history of soundtracks. This theme will plague us throughout the movie like a madness whose only virtue is persistence: it will not be forgotten. Da da da da da da . . . da da. This is a false gaiety. This is laughing when things ain't funny.

Porter: "Sorry for the gravediggers. Hard work in this frost."

Vienna: "Bombed about a bit." *The Third Man* is about the postwar four-power occupation of Vienna. Most of the film's contemporary viewers considered it a fairly accurate portrayal of Vienna, both visually and emotionally. The film's director, Carol Reed, used the piles of rubble, bombed-out houses, narrow streets and maze-like sewers. Inadvertently, he documented not only the place and time, but the metaphysical process by which the dislocations of WWII moved the West from the modern to the postmodern. It is visually and morally not unlike a much later and expressly postmodern movie, *Blade Runner*. Both are movies about a world of decay on top of which is the high-tech super-efficiency of the State. The police powers of occupied Vienna know with a cruel particularity what is the case personally and ideologically in every collapsed corner of the city. Information is for the first time depicted as more durable and more real than granite.

Martins: "I was going to stay with him but he died Thursday."

Mr. Crabbit: "Goodness that's awkward."

The Third Man: This title. Why is it so unsettling? There is you and I. Me and Dad. There is the familiar comfort of the dual. Reality and TV. But this movie is telling me that there is a third character, beyond my control, beyond my perception, mocking me. The third man is the closeted man. The man of whom no one may speak. It is taboo. He is there and not there. Unspeakable. He laughs from darkened recesses like the Shadow. (Isn't part of the perfection of Orson Welles as Harry Lime the resonance of Welles's earlier radio career as the Shadow?) Welles's figural entry in a darkened Viennese doorway trails ghosts in its wake.

The third man is our madness whispering to us, "Nothing is as it seems. Everything you think you know is false." The simplicity of this revelation is appalling. There is you and your father and then there is a third man! The third man is your real father. You want him, you want him to come forward, and yet you fear that if he does you will learn things you do not wish to know.

The Plot: Holly Martins, a simple American writer of westerns comes to Vienna at the request of his boyhood friend, and idol, Harry Lime. He discovers that Lime is dead. We follow Holly Martins's inept but dogged pursuit of the enigmatic "third man" who supposedly witnessed Lime's death, but who, as it turns out, is actually Lime himself. Along the way, Martins, played by Joseph Cotton, is assaulted by ever-more shocking revelations—that Lime may have been murdered, that Lime is actually alive, that Lime is a racketeer whose watered-down penicillin has crippled innumerable children. As Martins's investigation proceeds, he himself becomes increasingly at risk from Harry's gangster friends and perhaps even the police. Ironically, Martins's perseverance also does damage to innocent people around him: a porter, Sergeant Paine, and Harry himself are killed, all in the course of Martins's efforts to know the "true story." Worse yet, his investigation calls attention to Lime's girlfriend, Anna, with whom Holly has fallen in love. Now, because of Holly's inept presence, the Soviets are interested in her and her forged passport.

Colonel Calloway: "Death's at the bottom of everything, Martins. Leave death to the professionals."

Mozart Café: Baron Kurtz, one of Harry's friends who was at the scene of the "accident," has arranged to speak with Holly. He is a decadent Viennese straight out of the paintings of Klimt. (Because of the persistently canted camera angles, the film has a generally Expressionist feel. This is a world off-kilter. It is a world of dawning nausea.) Kurtz has a repulsive little dog and a repulsive homosexual relationship with Dr. Winkel ("Veenkel!"). But Baron Kurtz is also a "third man" because he is also Joseph Conrad's Kurtz. Is the conclusion one should draw from this that everybody is in hiding, even those in the open? Does everyone mask a "third" presence? Holly's pathetic third presence: the idealistic American hero, the "lone rider of Santa Fe." So this is a detective story about Holly who seeks the truth of the spritely dead by rummaging among the dried husks of the living. Is not the film's thesis then: all those who are alive are really dead (in the sense that they obscure their real selves)? And all those who are apparently dead are alive? Bizarrely, Anna's depressed comment, "I want to be dead too," indicates that she alone among these many characters is truly alive. She admits her falsity and is thus most true. (Holly: "Anything really wrong, Anna, with your papers?" Anna: "They're forged.")

Anna: "He said I laughed too much."

Casanova Club: Shots of Kurtz playing overripe melodies on his violin to an obscenely fat and ugly woman eating soup. A violent cynicism: the romantic and the oleaginous. Popescu: "Everyone ought to go careful in Vienna." Loud, lunatic, sobbing zither music.

The Reichsbrucke Bridge: Popescu arranges a meeting on this bridge to plot the murder of the porter. Looking hard, I catch my first sight of Lime—big, burly, great-coated, his back to the camera. My childhood self looks quickly to my father, "You?" "No, no, no. Pay attention."

Holly and Anna looking at a photograph.
Martins: "Harry?"
Anna, smiling: "Yes. He moved his head, but the rest is good isn't it?"

Harry's Street: The porter, who was about to spill Lime's secret to Holly, has been murdered. Holly enters a snarling crowd to find out what happened. Little Hansl arouses the crowd with his shrieks of "Papa, Papa." His childish words and gestures somehow imply that Martins is responsible. He is ominously round-faced like an avatar of Harry himself. He is a horrific dwarf, a goblin child, not quite human. If he is magically Lime's imp, then through him Harry attempts to lay the blame for his own murder of the porter on his best friend, Holly. The metaphysics of betrayal.

Lime: "How many dots, old man, could you afford?"

Cultural Center: Holly is kidnapped by a taxi driver. Is it one of Lime's thugs? "Are you going to kill me?" he shrieks. Comically, he is dumped out before the British Cultural Center where Mr. Crabbit has arranged for him to lecture on the "crisis of faith" in the modern novel. (Holly: "What's that?") Following his lecture, during which he is asked, "Where do you put Mr. James Joyce?", Martins is pursued by true murderers. He flees up a spiraling staircase, then down crumbling flights of concrete stairs. Stairs are everywhere in *The Third Man*, as if to provide access from one logic or metaphysic to another. At one level, Harry is a dear friend, at another a brutal criminal, at another a possessed child intent upon your death.

Police Headquarters: Holly learns the truth about Lime's penicillin racketeering.

Cabaret Bar: Martins drinks off his despair. Girls with pointy breasts dance before him. He doesn't notice. He takes no interest in pointy breasts. He buys two huge bunches of chrysanthemums from an old woman. Where do these chrysanthemums grow in frosty Vienna? Are these Eliot's flowers blossoming out of the dead land?

Martins: "Mind if I use that line in my next novel?"

Anna's Room: The poignancy of the truth: appropriate and available though Martins may be, Anna cannot love him. She prefers the memory of Harry to the reality of Holly. The full weight of Hollywood romantic conventions requires a coming-together of Anna and Holly. But Holly can never be anything more for her than Harry's slightly effeminate shadow. She is all worthiness loving the face of the utterly unworthy.

Holly stands at Anna's window hoping to see Lime. "He could be anybody." Holly doesn't see Harry, but he does see my father.

Certain though I am that it is he, I say nothing to my father. I do not insist on the obvious. I do not wish to hurt him with the obvious. I let the obvious pass. Let him claim what he likes. Let him tell me that he is the severe Colonel Calloway. Let him tell me that he is the glamorous Lime. I will nod and smile. I see all I need to see. I only wish that I could walk around that dark, dying Austrian corner with him, my arm around his shoulder. Just for the company.

Anna: "A person doesn't change because we find out more."

Anna's Street: Harry's first appearance. Holly sees his shoes in a darkened doorway. He takes them for the shoes of a police "tail." He shouts. A woman, awakened by the noise, turns on a second-story light. A slashing diagonal light illuminates Harry's smirking face. Carol Reed catches the flavor of the actual. Streets at night. Lime's shoes—hard, black and shiny. The surprise for the viewer is as fully emotional as we must imagine it is for Holly. Lime, in his all-black garb, mocks the idea of villainhood. He is cherubic and baby-faced. Is it not little Hansl?

One must wonder, however, what Harry's facial expressions mean. As always, Welles's portrayal borders on the excessive, the hambone high-school thespian. He looks surprised, quizzical, embarrassed, whimsical, pouty, sinister, menacing, and naughty in quick succession. Tiny, involuntary waves of emotion seem to ripple across his face.

As Martins approaches Harry, a truck comes between them, and when it has passed, Harry is gone. The echoing sound of Harry's fleeing shoes knocking on the Austrian cobblestones is the very sound of lonely despair. He sprints around the same corner at which Holly had earlier seen my father. And vanishes.

The Great Ferris Wheel: Vienna may be wrecked, but the Great Wheel is still functioning. Holly and Harry meet at it. They rise in one of its roomy cars high over the Prater. It also rises over Europe at mid-century. We are given a hawk's-eye view of the tragic scene.

The attractive and repulsive aspects of Harry's character lock in fierce antagonism. He is at once extravagant and tawdry, lighthearted and lethal. He is, in short, an American. His almost plausible logic: "Would you really feel any pity if one of those dots stopped moving forever? If I offered you

£20,000 for every dot that stops, would you really, old man, tell me to keep my money—or would you calculate how many dots you could afford to spare?"

(It is amazing to think of a time when one could "look out" on a world which stretched forth as panorama and veritable landscape. I suppose if Holly and Harry had had a TV in their Ferris wheel car, they could have looked out over America at end-century as well. Lime's depraved idea that people are just "dots" would then be nothing more than the bare fact of the matter. "Death? Don't be melodramatic, Holly. I'm not hurting anyone. Pixelated things don't feel pain. I'm just changing the channel, old man.")

Anna's Dresser Drawer: Lime is not the film's only dehumanizing force. When Colonel Calloway confiscates Anna's love letters from Harry, they are removed back to the station in one of Anna's dresser drawers. (Did they forget to bring a box? a paper bag?) But a close-up of the drawer at the station reveals that there are more than letters here. There is an unfinished embroidery, some small intimate boxes, sachets, and silky kerchiefs. This was all to be taken "downstairs" and "photographed." In the laboratory. Anna, too, is a "dot" for the police. There are no humans left in Vienna, only objects to be manipulated and calculated.

Sergeant Paine: "It's all right, Miss, we're like doctors."

The Trap: The film nears its conclusion. Holly waits in a café for Lime. He is conscious bait. He is betraying Harry. An exotic, perverse balloon seller approaches Calloway and Paine where they wait in darkened ambush. "Bahloon, mein herr?" The film becomes surreal. Who would imagine selling balloons in the midnight dark of a menacing side street? He wears a stagy beard. Is it the cunning Welles/Lime in disguise? Or is this a goofy role Reed found to humiliate my soldierly father?

Suddenly the music thunders in full theme: Harry Lime

makes his matchless entry, appearing in silhouette on top of the rubble that was a building, smoking a cigarette, coolly surveying the scene. He is king of the mountain. He is the last man standing. He is one ego aperch a ruined world. But it is the last moment of his grandeur. When he enters the café (gullibly, implausibly, fatally), there are instantaneous whistles and shouts. Dogs bark and sirens shrill. There is a sense of total mobilization. The entire police machinery of Vienna is unleashed on Harry. Ironically, the soldiers wear the helmets worn by the soldiers of the Third Reich. The scene has the appearance, so familiar from other movies of the period, of the SS in pursuit of a victim. Harry escapes, a frightened animal. Apparently, in this world, Nazis of one stripe pursue Nazis of another stripe. The trick is to persuade that there are differences between these "interests" or "zones."

Paine: "Sounds anti-British, Sir."

The Sewers: Suddenly we are tiny creatures, evil children, splashing in the bowels of this city. A great smell trickles here, cascades there. We are lost in a bewildering place: Harry Lime's home. He has escaped to his refuge in the sewers of Vienna. This foulness runs straight to the Blue Danube.

The cinematic effect is thrilling, bewildering. We are lost in this smelly labyrinth. Life cannot possibly live here. The background zither music is silent. There is only the rush of the sewer water and the desperate, lonely echo of Lime's running footsteps. I recognize it as the sound of the inside of my brain.

Lime comes to an open amphitheater, a central area where many smaller streams meet. He doesn't know which way to run. Voices, each seeming to speak a different language, burst from each tunnel. The languages swirl about him like ghosts. He can't run, but he runs.

Finally, Lime is shot during an exchange of fire with Calloway. He drags himself up one last flight of stairs, Martins just behind him, prepared to be Lime's executioner. But Lime has not yet accepted his death. He pulls himself up the metal stairs to a grill on the other side of which is the world. His fingers thrust through the grill. Abruptly, Reed moves the perspective to the street. We are looking at Harry's fingers emerging through the grill, cut off from the rest of his body. A dry wind rushes indifferently, as if these fingers really emerged from the floor of a desolate canyon. They wriggle hopelessly, pale worms. Grim cheese squeezed through a cloth. This is the truth, behind the world's daylit reality; its "business" is this despair. These detached fingers endowed with an awful will.

"That's it!"
"What?"
"That's it!"
"That's what?"
"Me!"
"You?"
"Me!"

"Those fingers?"

"Those fingers are my fingers! Orson Welles filmed the scene in the sewer weeks before and had returned to Italy where he was working on *Othello*. Mr. Reed needed fingers and I had some.

"Son, I played Harry Lime's fingers in *The Third Man*. There's something to tell your punk friends."

Should I have been happy for my father's brilliant past? Should I have applauded? Said, "Bravo, old man, kudos!"? Or should I have been appalled that these worm-like objects were his? I stared at him, his smiling, pleased face alternating in my immature mind with the image of his detached wriggling fingers.

One way or the other, that was that. We'd had our mythic evening. It was over with the startling and uncomfortable suddenness of emerging from the magic of a darkened theater into the afternoon sun or, worse yet, a suburban shopping mall. We'd shared. We'd talked. I'd discovered things about my father. But Anna's words kept returning to me: "A person doesn't change because you find out more." Too bad.

Unpredictably, my sisters had emerged from their emblematic poses and were now chattering on the couch with us. They didn't like the movie. It was boring. Why did we always have to watch shows with guns in them? More amazing yet, the general whirl of words and feelings was directing us toward the car, the '59 Dodge Sierra station wagon that sank into the street's tar like a dinosaur into the LaBrea. We were going to go "for a ride." It was to be a "family outing." Then you should have heard the din! Chaotic babble. Harry Lime had it good in those sewers. The tide of family feeling pushed us toward the street. When the car ignited, there was so much enthusiasm that we seemed to be boiling. We were going to blast off, all eight cylinders roaring. The instrument panel lights gave off a phosphorescent green glow in the darkness.

Then Janey said, "What about Mom?"

"Where's Mom?"

"Where has she been all these years?"

155

"She never does anything with us."

"Let's wait for her."

"Hey, here she comes!"

Indeed it was Mom, hopping across the lawn, laughing, catching up. Finally, it appeared that we were a happy family. What was there to dread in this world? She got in the backseat with my sisters. I could hear them popping like popcorn. But there was also the curious scent that invariably indicated that a few kernels were scorching at the bottom of the pan. I looked back.

In the nervous dark of our family station wagon's backseat I could see the telltale glow of my mother's hair. It was on fire. She had it up in a sort of fetching beehive of embers. It was a torch. It was roaring. But no one seemed to notice but me. Little wisps of charred film floated in the air.

"Roll down your window a little, Butch, it's getting hot in here."

I did as I was told but then looked quickly back again. They were laughing and talking rapidly. They might have been college roommates. But already the torch of my mother's hair had been passed. Janey's brown hair flamed. Winny's blonde hair smoldered. I turned forward.

"Dad . . ."

"What?"

"There's something wrong."

"Like what?" He accelerated. The bleary ooze of tire emerged from the smeary ooze of road. The speedometer struggled forward. We snapped outward. I was pushed back against the seat. We were blasting off for Mars. (Would Holly the Martian meet us there?) I turned again, hoping against hope that I'd been seeing things. I was greeted by three smiles and a solid hedge of flaming brow.

"What are you lookin' at?" they cried together, socking each other in the arm at the hilarious coincidence.

I looked forward. The little toy homes flew by on each side, illuminated by their ridiculously frail porch lights. If someone somewhere, some superior force, were centrifuging our suburb, what liquid would trickle from us?

"Well?" my father asked. "What is it?"

"Nothin'."

Georganne Rundbald

Curtis White, born in 1951, is the author of *Heretical Songs* (1951), *Metaphysics in the Midwest* (1988), *The Idea of Home* (1992), *Anarcho-Hindu* (1995), and *Monstrous Possibility* (1998).

DALKEY ARCHIVE PAPERBACKS

FELIPE ALFAU, *Chromos.*
    Locos.
    Sentimental Songs.
ALAN ANSEN,
    Contact Highs: Selected Poems 1957-1987.
DJUNA BARNES, *Ladies Almanack.*
    Ryder.
JOHN BARTH, *LETTERS.*
    Sabbatical.
ANDREI BITOV, *Pushkin House.*
ROGER BOYLAN, *Killoyle.*
CHRISTINE BROOKE-ROSE, *Amalgamemnon.*
GERALD BURNS, *Shorter Poems.*
MICHEL BUTOR,
    Portrait of the Artist as a Young Ape.
JULIETA CAMPOS, *The Fear of Losing Eurydice.*
ANNE CARSON, *Eros the Bittersweet.*
LOUIS-FERDINAND CÉLINE, *Castle to Castle.*
    North.
    Rigadoon.
HUGO CHARTERIS, *The Tide Is Right.*
JEROME CHARYN, *The Tar Baby.*
EMILY HOLMES COLEMAN, *The Shutter of Snow.*
ROBERT COOVER, *A Night at the Movies.*
STANLEY CRAWFORD,
    Some Instructions to My Wife.
RENÉ CREVEL, *Putting My Foot in It.*
RALPH CUSACK, *Cadenza.*
SUSAN DAITCH, *Storytown.*
PETER DIMOCK,
    A Short Rhetoric for Leaving the Family.
COLEMAN DOWELL, *Island People.*
    Too Much Flesh and Jabez.
RIKKI DUCORNET, *The Fountains of Neptune.*
    The Jade Cabinet.
    Phosphor in Dreamland.
    The Stain.

WILLIAM EASTLAKE, *Lyric of the Circle Heart.*
STANLEY ELKIN, *The Dick Gibson Show.*
ANNIE ERNAUX, *Cleaned Out.*
LAUREN FAIRBANKS, *Muzzle Thyself.*
    Sister Carrie.
LESLIE A. FIEDLER,
    Love and Death in the American Novel.
RONALD FIRBANK, *Complete Short Stories.*
FORD MADOX FORD, *The March of Literature.*
JANICE GALLOWAY, *Foreign Parts.*
    The Trick Is to Keep Breathing.
WILLIAM H. GASS,
    Willie Masters' Lonesome Wife.
C. S. GISCOMBE, *Giscome Road.*
    Here.
KAREN ELIZABETH GORDON, *The Red Shoes.*
GEOFFREY GREEN, ET AL, *The Vineland Papers.*
PATRICK GRAINVILLE, *The Cave of Heaven.*
JOHN HAWKES, *Whistlejacket.*
ALDOUS HUXLEY, *Antic Hay.*
    Point Counter Point.
    Those Barren Leaves.
    Time Must Have a Stop.
TADEUSZ KONWICKI, *The Polish Complex.*
EWA KURYLUK, *Century 21.*
OSMAN LINS,
    The Queen of the Prisons of Greece.
ALF MAC LOCHLAINN,
    The Corpus in the Library.
    Out of Focus.
D. KEITH MANO, *Take Five.*
BEN MARCUS, *The Age of Wire and String.*
DAVID MARKSON, *Collected Poems.*
    Reader's Block.
    Springer's Progress.
    Wittgenstein's Mistress.
CARL R. MARTIN, *Genii Over Salzburg.*

DALKEY ARCHIVE PAPERBACKS

Dalkey Archive Press
ISU Box 4241, Normal, IL 61790–4241
fax (309) 438–7422
Visit our website at www.cas.ilstu.edu/english/dalkey/dalkey.html